MVFOL

D1051598

schooled in
revenge

schooled in
revenge

JESSE LASKY

HYPERION

NEW YORK

Revenge © 2013 ABC Studios. All Rights Reserved.

All rights reserved. No part of this book may be used or reproduced
in any manner whatsoever without the written permission of the
Publisher. Printed in the United States of America. For information
address Hyperion, 1500 Broadway, New York, New York 10036.

Library of Congress Cataloging-in-Publication Data

Lasky, Jesse.
   Schooled in Revenge / Jesse Lasky. — First edition.
       pages   cm
ISBN 978-1-4013-1110-0
   1. Revenge —Fiction.   2. Napa (Calif.) —Fiction.   3. Radio and
television novels.   I. Revenge (Television program)   II. Title.
   PS3612.A859S36 2013
   813'.6 —dc23

                                2013012432

FIRST EDITION

10 9 8 7 6 5 4 3 2

THIS LABEL APPLIES TO TEXT STOCK

We try to produce the most beautiful books possible, and we are also
extremely concerned about the impact of our manufacturing process
on the forests of the world and the environment as a whole. Accordingly, we've made sure that all of the paper we use has been certified as
coming from forests that are managed, to ensure the protection of the
people and wildlife dependent upon them.

To all of those who have ever been
wronged . . . and so desperately wanted
to make it right

If you prick us do we not bleed?
If you tickle us do we not laugh?
If you poison us do we not die?
And if you wrong us shall we not revenge?

—SHAKESPEARE, *The Merchant of Venice*

schooled in
revenge

CHAPTER ONE

A VA WINTERS LOOKED OUT THE WINDOW OF THE charter plane, taking in the desolate landscape below as the pilot banked toward a small patch of level land. Rebun Island, Japan, was even more remote than she had expected, the tiny landing strip surrounded on three sides by snow-covered cliffs and fronted by the frigid waters of the Rebun Channel.

Then again, she hadn't expected it to be easy. She knew what she was signing up for when she'd accepted Takeda's offer of training.

The plane touched down, bouncing over the frozen ground until it finally came to a stop. A minute later, the door opened and Ava exited with her small duffel bag in one gloved hand.

"Welcome to Japan," the pilot said, stepping to the ground beside her.

"Thank you." She turned her attention to the surrounding landscape, the wind whipping her long dark hair around her face. There was no airport, no taxi station, no people. She looked at the pilot, already heading back into the plane. "Wait! Where do I go from here?"

He glanced back, nodding at something behind her.

She turned around, peering into the distance until she could make out a building at the top of the jagged cliffs, the sea crashing violently against the rocks at its feet.

"But . . . how am I supposed to get there?" Ava asked.

"If you want this badly enough," the pilot said, climbing into the plane and reaching for the door, "you will find a way."

She was still in shock when the propellers began to move. For a minute, she could only watch as the plane took off into the steely sky. The hum of its engine had diminished to a faint buzz when a frigid wind blew in from the Rebun Channel, sending a shock of cold through her system. She shivered, pulling up the hood of her sweatshirt, and started walking.

The ground was icy, her warm breath turning to smoke as it hit the frigid air. Frost blanketed the cliffs in front of her but she kept her eyes on the ground, not wanting to trip and fall. She'd come to the island with a singular goal. An injury was the last thing she needed this early in the game.

After two hours of struggling to stay upright on the frozen soil, she finally reached the base of the cliff. Pausing to catch her breath, she tipped her head back, her gaze coming to rest on the old Japanese *tera* forty feet above her. She scanned the face of the cliff, hoping for some kind of hidden staircase, or at the very least, something resembling toeholds.

But there was nothing. Just a wall of sheer rock.

Taking a deep breath, she slung the duffel bag over her shoulder and across her chest, adjusting the strap so it fit snugly against her body. Then she started to climb. At first, she could hardly see the small crevices that could be used as footholds, the protruding rock she could use to pull herself upward. But after a while, her eyes became accustomed to scanning for the next indentation, the next thing to grab. As darkness began to seep across the sky, she became aware of her aching arms and forced herself to move faster. She didn't have the luxury of hanging by her fingers, looking for the perfect place to put her feet.

The past had toughened her will, but she only had so much upper-body strength.

She was near the top when her foot slipped, a smattering of rocks falling into the abyss below as she clung to the cliff face, her breath coming fast and heavy, her heart nearly pounding out of her chest. She allowed herself only a minute to gather her courage before she started climbing again.

Her arms and legs were trembling when she finally heaved herself over the top of the cliff. She lay there for a minute, sweat coating her body despite the frigid temperatures. When she could breathe without gasping, she got to her feet and headed for the tera.

It was smaller than it had looked from the ground, and less imposing, with five pillars resting atop a gently curved roof. She'd read somewhere that it was a tradition of this kind of architecture, the pillars representing the Buddhist universe's central elements: sky, wind, fire, water, and earth. The roof was a deep red, a punctuation mark against the snow-covered terrain.

But it was too cold to stand still, and she grabbed on to a bamboo pillar, one of many lining the walkway to the tera's entrance, and walked toward two large doors at the front of the building. She was almost there, her steps slowing to a shuffle, when exhaustion overtook her. She dropped to her knees, closing her eyes and trying to find the strength to stand.

"You're Ava Winters," a voice said from behind her.

Ava turned in surprise, her gaze landing on a red-haired woman about her age. Ava tried to smile around the pain in her arms and legs, thinking the woman had come to greet her, but she only favored Ava with a steely glare before walking wordlessly past her.

Too tired to care, Ava got to her feet. She was inching her way forward when the doors to the tera opened. A stoic, authoritative man with a weathered face and strong build stood in the doorway. He said something to her in Japanese as the wind howled around them. She had no idea what the words meant, but it didn't matter.

This was Satoshi Takeda.

An aura of strength and control emanated from him, temporarily stopping her forward progress. A moment later, she remembered why she had come.

She met his gaze. "Takeda."

Silence settled between them. Even the wind seemed to calm in the face of his presence.

Finally, he nodded.

Ava bowed. "I'm ready to start my training."

CHAPTER TWO

Ava sits across from her grandmother, morning sun flooding the south dining hall of the Napa Valley Country Club. Ava is fourteen years old, and while she loves coming to the club with her grandmother, it doesn't dim the recent loss of her parents.

Her grandmother gazes with concern at Ava's untouched plate. "Ava, you must eat. I know it's hard, but your parents would want you to be healthy and well. You know that, don't you?"

Ava hears the worry in her grandmother's voice and picks up her fork. "Sometimes I don't remember them," she says guiltily, forcing a bite of poached egg into her mouth.

"That's what I'm here for, my dear," her grandmother says gently. "To remind you." She reaches across the table to squeeze Ava's free hand. "And the vineyard will remind you, too. Every breeze. Every harvest. Every vine."

Ava musters a smile. Just thinking about the vineyard brings her comfort. Her parents may be gone, but their presence lingers in the soil at Starling, in the wine aging in barrels in the cellar, the wind rustling the vines. As long as Ava has it, they'll always be near.

Ava is taking another bite, feeling the tiniest bit better, when a man approaches her grandmother. Tall and distinguished, his hair frosted with silver, he's wearing a suit and tie despite the fact that it's Sunday and quite warm. He pulls out the chair and joins them almost before her grandmother can register his presence.

"Hello, Sylvie," the man says. "Looking lovely as ever."

Ava's grandmother looks up, her elegant features turning into an emotionless mask. "I'd ask what you want, Mr. Reinhardt, but I've never been one for pretenses."

The man's laugh is brittle. "One of the things I admire about you."

She waves a hand in dismissal. "You have my answer; I will never sell Starling. There's nothing else to be said about the matter."

The man named Reinhardt nods. "So you've said." He reaches across the table, plucking an apple from the bowl of fruit at its center. He bites into it, his gaze falling on Ava.

"You know the story of Adam and Eve, don't you, sweetheart? About the apple in the Garden of Eden?"

Ava's eyes slide to her grandmother before she looks back at the man and nods.

"Do you know what made Eve want the apple so badly?"

Ava thinks about it, wanting to get the answer right, although she could not have said why. "Because the devil tricked her?" she suggests shyly.

The man sets the fruit down, dabbing at his mouth with one of the linen napkins. "Because she was told she couldn't *have it." The man's expression hardens. "And that just made her want it more."*

THE SKY WAS STILL PAINTED WITH PINK AND OR-ange when Ava arrived at the training area behind the tera. She had hardly slept, the ghosts of her past swirling through the haze of half-sleep until she couldn't be sure if she was awake or dreaming. She was glad to be outside, glad to finally begin her journey. Sleep wouldn't come easy until her demons were exorcised.

The training room was about a half mile behind the tera. A smaller version of the main house, the structure was surrounded on three sides by large stone walls. The fourth side needed no marker. It ended at the edge of the cliff, overlooking the far-reaching sea.

It wasn't as cold as it had been the day before, but that wasn't saying much. It was still a million times colder than Napa. Ava forced herself not to think about it. Cold was minor compared to what she had endured, compared to what she was willing to endure to see vengeance served.

She entered the training area through a wooden door, surprised to find a powerfully built man with short sandy hair already inside.

"Hi," Ava said quietly, unsure about the rules and customs of their training.

He nodded. "Hey."

She stepped forward, extending a hand. "I'm Ava Winters, resident new kid."

He chuckled, taking her hand, his brown eyes guarded. "Jon West. And I thought I was the new kid."

"It's your first day, too?" Ava asked.

"It is," he confirmed. There was something dark behind his confident gaze, and a powerful current of attraction flooded Ava's body as his eyes held hers.

Before she could respond, another guy, tall and lean, burst into the room, Reena, the flinty-eyed redhead from the night before, at his side.

"The newbies have arrived!" he exclaimed, opening his arms magnanimously.

"You're such an asshole, Cruz." Reena rolled her eyes affectionately before smiling at him. "I like that about you."

Their exchange was familiar, like they'd replayed the same scene many times before.

The guy named Cruz gave Reena a slow grin, the chemistry between them a palpable presence in the room.

A moment later, Takeda stepped through the weathered door, his expression solemn. Cruz immediately fell in line next to Reena, his lighthearted demeanor gone. After a brief hesitation, Ava and Jon followed suit, taking their cues from the more experienced students. They watched Takeda reverently as he paced in front of them.

"Revenge," Takeda began, "is not a swift blow to the skull or the simple pull of a trigger, although you will learn these things in the event that something goes awry in your quest. Rather, revenge is death by a thousand cuts, a slow and calculated process to make your enemies suffer as you have. This is not cruelty. It is a restoration of justice, of balance."

Takeda stopped in front of Ava, meeting her eyes as if he was speaking only to her.

"You must dedicate yourself to revenge. It is not a hobby.

Not a part-time pursuit. It will consume you. It will engulf you. But with my guidance, it will also empower you."

Faces flashed across Ava's mind. Charlie. William Reinhardt.

And everyone who helped them take what was hers.

"Together we will map a course to bring justice to every person who has wronged you," Takeda continued, resuming his pacing in front of the group. "But to exact revenge without preparation is suicide, and first among these preparations is control. You must learn to control your emotions, your mind, your body, so that you may act with a clear head and a focused heart. I will teach you this control."

Takeda's words were still ringing through the training room when the door opened and a young woman stepped in quietly. Slender, with long blond hair twisted into a loose braid, she looked even younger than Ava. Somehow the scar that ran across one cheek only added to her fragile beauty. Eyes downcast, she took up a position apart from Ava and the others.

Ava refocused on Takeda as he stopped in front of Jon, placing a hand on his shoulder.

"Revenge is not an option. It is a need. A burning desire to right the wrongs of those who have taken someone from you."

Daring a glance at Jon, Ava was surprised to see his impassive expression turn steely. Is that why he was here? Because someone had been taken from him?

Takeda walked farther down the line, stopping in front of Cruz. "To right the wrongs of those who have crossed you . . ." Cruz stared straight ahead, unflinching, as Takeda continued to Reena. "To right the wrongs of those who have destroyed everything without consequence. Without remorse." He gazed at each of them as he made his way back to Ava. When he spoke again, his words seemed meant just for her. "Revenge is a room with an entrance but no exit. Are you ready to walk inside?"

CHAPTER THREE

Flashbulbs pop, unrelenting as twenty-four-year-old Reena walks out of notorious Los Angeles hot spot Lily's Lounge holding a martini glass in one hand and a second martini glass in the other. It's only 2 p.m., but as the cliché goes, it's five o'clock somewhere, and Reena never misses an opportunity to cause a scene.

It's what the paparazzi love best about her.

"Reena! Reena! What's your mother going to say?" one of the tabloid journalists calls out, waiting on the bustling boulevard outside to snap as many photos as he can of her.

"The senator has bigger things to worry about than me," Reena scoffs as she spills gin all over herself, stepping into a decadent black limousine.

She's rash and reckless, but okay with it. All of it. She doesn't need structure, just an open bar.

"Do you think your mother will get reelected?" the vultures shout.

Reena downs her drink and puts on her large sunglasses. "Dunno. That would mean I was paying attention."

REENA SLAMMED THE WOODEN BOW INTO THE dense, frigid sand as Cruz jumped away, narrowly escaping the blow.

They were on the beach below the tera. Takeda and the other students stood off to the side, observing Reena and Cruz's training exercise.

"Pay attention to the moves he hasn't yet made," Takeda advised. "Your rage distracts you."

The criticism got under Reena's skin, raising her ire even as she continued to circle Cruz, looking for another opportunity to gain the upper hand.

"My rage is what fuels me!" she shouted.

She swung the bow behind her back, using the momentum to bring it forward, nailing Cruz in the thigh. He dropped to the ground in pain, grunting in frustration as Reena walked over his fallen body to place her bow in front of Takeda.

"You lack sympathy," Takeda stated.

Reena walked toward the others, Takeda's words echoing in her ears. She assumed it was a compliment, but there was something in the way he said it that made her wonder. She fell in line, the waves just reaching her bare toes. Reena gritted her teeth against the frigid water. Physical discomfort she could endure.

It was knowing that no one had paid for her mother's death that was unbearable.

She pushed the thought away. She was taking steps to remedy the situation. It's why she was here. She had to focus. And even her feelings for Cruz couldn't get in the way.

She watched as Jon bent down, picking up Cruz's bow from

the sand near his feet. He walked over to where Cruz lay, still recovering from Reena's blow, and offered him a hand.

Cruz reached past Jon's hand, grabbing his arm instead and flipping him onto the harsh sand. "Sorry, dude. You lose."

Even Reena didn't see it coming, and that was saying something. She knew Cruz almost as well as he knew himself.

Cruz bounced up, standing over Jon with a look of triumph on his face.

Takeda shook his head. "Vengeance may not reside with pity," he says. "Only one may win. You must decide which is most important. To have pity for your opponent is to give them an advantage. You must distance yourself from emotion," Takeda further advised. "It will get in the way, it will make you weak."

Takeda was speaking to them all, but Reena felt her face flush with the words. It was no secret that she and Cruz had a relationship. But her feelings for him went far beyond that of a lover. He was her best friend. The only person who really knew who she was. The only person who had been with her both before and after her mother's death. Who knew how she suffered.

Cruz was a part of her. Whatever Takeda said, she would find a way to balance her feelings for him with her desire for revenge.

"But our emotions are what brought us here," Ava said.

Reena fought the urge to roll her eyes. They were all novices in revenge, but Ava gave new meaning to the word *amateur*. It was obvious that she was too naïve. Too soft. Training to fight and speak other languages was the least of her problems.

JESSE LASKY

"But it is here you must leave them when you one day head back out into the world," Takeda responded. He turned and walked away, signaling their break.

They waited for him to clear the beach before breaking formation. Reena was turning to say something to Cruz when she caught Ava staring quizzically at her.

"Is there a problem?" Reena asked, narrowing her eyes.

Ava shook her head. "No problem, it's just . . ."

"It's just *what*?" Reena demanded.

"I recognize you," Ava said. "At least, I think I do. You're Reena Fuller. The daughter of that senator. The one who was killed."

A chill ran through Reena's body. She knew her mother was dead. Had lived with the reality of it for a long time. But she hated hearing someone say it out loud. Especially someone she didn't know.

"I'm sorry," Ava continued, placing a gentle hand on Reena's arm. "I didn't mean to upset you. My parents died, too, in a car accident."

As if that mattered. As if that somehow made it better. The words didn't even begin to thaw the ice around Reena's heart.

"Yeah, well, this wasn't an accident." She picked up her bow, stalking for the path leading to the tera.

CHAPTER FOUR

Walking through the tasting room at Starling Vineyards, Ava is warmly welcomed by Napa mainstays, vintners, and a multitude of tourists who've come to experience the wine country's most esteemed establishment. The repurposed wood of the colonial-style space coordinates perfectly with the mustard-seed bar tops and café tables where patrons sip and savor.

Ava pours a healthy glass of Pinot Gris for a young couple sitting on the plush bar stools.

"Aren't starlings those birds that defend their nests to the death?" the young man cracks as he drinks his wine.

"Stop flirting," his wife warns with a laugh.

"Leave me alone," he says. "I'm making small talk with the heiress to the Starling throne."

Ava laughs, offering the lady another glass.

"To the death, huh?" says an Englishman sitting a few feet away. "But it's just a nest."

She looks at him coolly. "Well, the nest is their home. And home is . . ."

"Let me guess, where the heart is?" he jokes, his shaggy

hair a boyish contrast to his chiseled jaw and striking cheek-bones.

Ava nods, feeling an instant physical attraction to him. She takes out a glass, asking if he'd prefer red or white.

"Actually, how about your name instead?" the man says.

"Ava Winters," she responds, selecting a nice red.

"Why that one?" he asks, tipping his head at the bottle.

"Red wine often goes through a process called fining," she explains. "It corrects the wine's faults." She smirks at him. "Looks like you could use some fining yourself."

"Touché," the man laughs. He extends a hand. "I'm Charles. Charles Bay. You can call me Charlie."

He removes a brochure from his jacket pocket. On the cover is a photo of Ava with an older woman, the two of them sitting by a large marble fountain in front of Starling Vineyards.

"Nice picture," he says.

Ava chuckles, embarrassed.

"So is it true?" he asks her.

"Is what true?"

He waves his arm expansively. "That all of this is going to be yours one day."

Ava nods. "I suppose so."

Charlie sips the Cabernet she poured for him. "What's your favorite part?"

"About what?"

"About all of it; Napa, your vineyard . . ."

Ava thinks about the question as she reaches into a small bucket. She pulls out a souvenir key chain with a dangling cork, the words STARLING VINEYARDS, NAPA VALLEY, CA embedded on it in black ink.

Ava hands it to him. "The little things."

Charlie regards her with a slow smile. "Would you care to join me for a drink?"

"I can't," Ava says, feeling a twinge of regret. "Not with all these customers around."

"Then after you're done working," he says insistently. "There's a pub just a few blocks from here. What do you say?"

"Actually," Ava says, embarrassed all over again, "I won't turn twenty-one for another six months."

He smiles his understanding. "A rain check, then?"

"How do you know you'll still be around?" she asks.

Charlie smiles. So does she. And it's suddenly clear that he will.

A VA WAS STANDING ON THE EDGE OF THE CLIFF when she heard someone approach from behind.

Turning toward the footsteps, Ava was surprised to see Jon. "Couldn't sleep?" he asked, stopping beside her.

Pulling her robe more tightly around her body, she looked back out over the water. It was after midnight, the ocean endless and inky under a clear sky blanketed with stars. It was desolate, feral. And very, very beautiful.

"I'd always dreamed of coming to Japan. Seeing this part of the world," she murmured. "But not like this."

"I know what you mean," Jon said beside her. He seemed to hesitate. "Why does he do this? Takeda? What does he get out of it?"

She glanced over at him. His arms were crossed in front of his chest, his biceps bulging from the sleeves of his T-shirt. He was wearing shorts, as unprepared for the cold as Ava.

"You didn't ask that question before you came here to train?" she asked.

"I was too busy loving the idea of retribution."

His smile was wry, but Ava shivered as he spoke the word. Retribution. Justice. Revenge. Whatever its name, it was what drove her as well.

"I don't know Takeda's reasons," she said. "And I don't really care. I'm here to focus on my own."

Jon nodded, turning his gaze back to the water. "Probably for the best."

She sighed. "Look, I'm sorry. I didn't mean that to be bitchy."

He chuckled. "Not at all. You're here to work. I get it. And you're right; we all have our reasons for being here. Takeda's don't really have anything to do with us."

"What are your reasons for being here?" Ava asked, turning to him. "If you don't mind my asking, that is."

"Ava . . . ," he began.

She caught the hesitation in his voice and was embarrassed by her pushiness. She smiled. "You know what? I'm sorry." She laughed a little. "I don't know what I was thinking. It's none of my business why you're here. I think I've been out of the social loop too long. I don't even know how to talk to anyone anymore."

He shook his head. "No apology necessary. I guess I'm still getting my head around everything that happened . . . everything that led me here. Another time?"

She smiled, nodding. "Sure."

He held her gaze, a current of warmth moving between them. Ava was still caught in his brown eyes when she noticed movement in her peripheral vision. Someone was moving toward them from the shadows. As the figure came closer, Ava saw that it was a woman, tall and slender, her blond hair a glimmer in the moonlight.

She stepped next to them, although slightly apart, and turned her attention to the sea.

"This was where I used to come, too," she said.

"Who are you?" Ava asked.

The woman hesitated before turning her striking brown eyes on Ava. "My name is Emily Thorne."

CHAPTER FIVE

E MILY CROSSED HER ARMS ACROSS HER CHEST, HER blond hair billowing out behind her like a handful of flaxen ribbon.

"I spent so many nights here, trying to find some kind of comfort, some kind of peace." She gave them a small smile. "It never really worked. But still . . . it beat tossing and turning."

Ava was surprised by the revelation. "You've been here before, then?" she asked.

Emily nodded. "I trained with Takeda a long time ago."

There was something strong and dignified in the way she held herself, like she'd weathered more than one storm. Ava wondered what had brought Emily to Rebun Island in the first place—and what had brought her back.

"Why did you come back?" Jon asked, as if he were tapped directly into Ava's brain.

A wall seemed to drop over Emily's face, her expression unreadable. This was someone very accustomed to keeping to herself.

"I have my reasons," she said cryptically.

A ferocious breath of the night air sent shivers down Ava's

spine. Even Jon shook a little with the cold. Emily didn't seem to notice it at all.

"And did it help?" Ava asked, following Emily's gaze out over the sea. "Coming out here at night when you couldn't sleep?"

Emily smiled a little. "Sometimes. Mostly, it just takes time."

"Does that mean it gets better?" Ava wanted—needed—to know.

Emily didn't answer right away, and for a minute Ava wondered if her words had been snatched by the wind before they could reach Emily's ears. But a moment later, Emily glanced at her, brown eyes shining in the faint light of the moon.

"I'm still trying to figure that out," she said.

She gave them a small nod and headed for the tera.

"So then this is the right thing to do." The words were out of Ava's mouth before she could stop them.

Emily stopped, turning toward Ava and Jon. "The people who wronged you, do they deserve to pay for what they've done?" The question was matter-of-fact, Emily's voice even, as she fixed her eyes unflinchingly on Ava and Jon.

They nodded.

She gave them a knowing look. "Then how can their punishment be anything but justice?"

She turned and walked away, the darkness swallowing her whole.

CHAPTER SIX

RAIN PELTED AVA'S FACE AS SHE AND REENA TRIED to maintain their balance above the rocky shores of the channel. Above, the sky was gray, offering little light or warmth, and the sea smacked violently against the base of the cliffs below as the women tried to steady their hands and feet on the indents in the cliff face.

Ava had been at Rebun Island for almost a month and had easily fallen into the routine: sleep, eat, train. Sometimes training was working with the wooden bows on the sandy beach. Other times it was sparring with a foil or climbing the cliff using the ropes that dangled there. Sometimes they stayed indoors, conversing in Japanese or discussing the psychology of their mission.

The psychology of revenge.

It consumed every waking minute and every sleeping one, too, the ghosts of Ava's past chased through her dreams by the promise of retribution.

Ava's mind and body were changing, her muscles becoming leaner and stronger, her mind becoming clearer and more focused. Even Reena had become more cautious in her treatment of Ava—both in and out of the training room. As if she sensed the change in Ava and knew the day was coming when Ava wouldn't take her shit.

"If you cannot change your surroundings, you must find a way to control them," Takeda instructed, standing on the cliff above the beach with the scarred young woman who joined them in their exercises but never spoke.

Ava grabbed hold of a rock, hoisting herself toward one of the ropes. She and Reena were in a dead heat, both of them dangling above the stormy channel while Jon and Cruz climbed above them, each with a white flag on his back. They had started on the beach, the men given a slight head start as they began their ascent. The women were supposed to retrieve one of the flags before the men reached the top of the cliff, and Ava and Reena were both determined to win, working their way furiously up the cliff face despite the punishing wind and rain.

Forgoing the ropes for speed, Reena scrabbled for whatever she could find protruding from the cliff, gaining on Jon fast enough to take a swipe at his flag. She missed, and the momentum of her reach caused her to lose her balance. For one terrifying moment, Ava stopped climbing, watching as Reena scrambled for something to hold on to before her hand finally closed around one of the ropes. She cursed, swinging wildly in the air as Ava resumed her climb.

Suddenly, the gray skies opened up with a violent clap of thunder, the rain intensifying to a roar that made it difficult to hear Takeda's instructions.

"Remain steady as the world around you falls into chaos," Takeda called out calmly, standing without shelter on the cliff ledge above.

Ava's arms screamed in pain, her legs aching from the work of balancing her body on the vertical cliff face. But Reena was still swinging, still regrouping from her near fall. For a few seconds, Ava was mesmerized by the small circle tattooed on the back of Reena's neck, visible under her ponytail as she swung back and forth in front of the cliff.

Ava refocused. This was her chance to gain an advantage, and she forced herself to move faster, pushing her body to its limit as she climbed toward Cruz.

She was so close she could see the treads in his shoes when she took a swipe at his flag, but it was a miscalculation, and she missed, although thankfully she didn't lose her footing.

Angry with herself for being impatient, for not waiting until the time was right, Ava shoved her foot harshly into a crevice on the cliffside and let go of the rope. She grabbed on to the rocks, slick with rain and something that felt suspiciously like ice. She wanted to wipe the water, running in rivulets from her hair and forehead, from her face, but she needed both hands.

She heard Takeda's voice from another exercise: *Obstacles are not bad. They are not good. They simply are. Do not see them as your enemy but as necessary steps in your journey.*

She pushed the thought of the rain from her mind and kept climbing, focusing on keeping a sure hand, a steady foothold, on the rocks as she made her way upward. A bolt of lightning streaked across the sky followed by an earsplitting strike of thunder.

"Do not be rattled," Takeda intoned. "And expect to be surprised."

Ava glanced over at Reena, unsurprised to see that she was back in the game, using one of the ropes to climb toward Jon, who was moving rapidly toward the top of the cliff. He was fast, faster even than Cruz. Ava turned her attention to Cruz, a more reachable target.

A minute later, Reena's shout found its way through the rain. "Son of a bitch!"

Ava glanced over, unable to suppress the grin that rose to her lips as she watched Jon pull himself over the top of the cliff.

She stopped watching and started moving again when Reena turned her attention to Cruz, the only remaining target.

"Want me? Gonna have to catch me!" Cruz called, hanging on to one of the drenched ropes as he climbed.

Ava couldn't be sure if he was just slow or if he was so cocky that he wasn't in a hurry, but she was gaining on him. And so was Reena. Cruz was positioned between them, Ava slightly ahead of Reena as they all approached the top of the cliff. Taking a chance, Ava pushed off with her feet, clinging to the rope as she swung toward Cruz, reaching out to try to take the flag as she came close to him. She felt the silky fabric of the flag in her fingers for a split second before she lost her grip on it, swinging back and crashing into the solid rock.

Damn it! There was no way Reena was going to win.

Another lightning bolt momentarily illuminated the sky as the rain teemed harder. Cruz, now evenly situated between Ava and Reena, steadied himself and continued to climb.

"Embrace the challenges of the task at hand," Takeda reminded them. "In revenge, obstacles must be thought of as guideposts, guideposts that can help you figure out the proper course. To find a way around these guideposts requires you to take the path others have not."

The words rang in Ava's ear, the rain suddenly fading into the background as her mind grasped for the seed planted by Takeda's words. A moment later, she had it, and she reached for one of the loose rocks on a protruding boulder near her right hand.

"Hey, Reena! Something in your eye?"

Reena glanced over, and her gaze came to rest on the rock in Ava's hand. She flinched, ducking, and Cruz turned his back on Ava, positioning himself to protect Reena from possible assault. In that moment, his flag was completely exposed.

Ava reached out and took it, clambering up the last few feet of the cliff with renewed energy. Heaving herself over the edge of the cliff, she dropped onto her back. Her clothes were soaked through and stuck to her skin, but euphoria hummed through her veins. For the first time in a long time, she felt in control.

Cruz and Reena pulled themselves up over the ledge, and everyone lay there in silence, catching their breath. A couple of minutes later, they got to their feet and assumed formation in front of Takeda.

He walked down the line, surveying them calmly as if the rain weren't still soaking them all to the bone. Stopping in front of Ava, he surveyed her with clinical eyes.

She bowed, offering him Cruz's white flag. "Sensei."

Takeda nodded, accepting the flag. "You knew Cruz would protect Reena, didn't you?"

"Yes, Sensei," she answered quietly.

"He cares for her," Takeda said. "Now you see how that gets in the way." He turned his attention to the group, speaking loud enough for everyone to hear. "How it makes you weak. How it makes you vulnerable."

They were standing in the wake of his silence when a harsh ring cut through the air.

Takeda removed a satellite phone from his belt and walked a few feet away, turning his back on them. His voice was low but not inaudible.

"May first? That's less than five weeks away." A pause as he listened to the person on the other end of the phone. "Then we don't have much time."

He hung up and returned to the group, but Ava's mind was reeling. She didn't know what May first meant to Takeda, but it meant only one thing to her: the Annual Starling Vineyards Gala.

CHAPTER SEVEN

A band marches steadily on the pavement outside the California State Capitol in Sacramento as a crowd of thousands rallies enthusiastically, police stationed around barricades to keep them at bay.

But Reena isn't paying attention to the crowd. She's too busy flirting with Cruz Benton, her mother's chief staff assistant.

"I like your hair up like that," he says, appraising her.

She's not buying the smooth-talker routine, but at least he's cute. "My mom says it makes me look older, but I think she means boring."

Cruz grins. "Boring is probably the idea."

She holds up her smartphone, revealing the home page for popular gossip website EyeCandyCorn.com, a photo of a hard-partying Reena guzzling a bottle of Dom Perignon.

"I take it you're referring to my extracurricular activities?"

He opens his mouth to speak but is cut off by the roar of applause as Reena's mother, lean and elegant in a white pant-suit that accentuates her dark hair, takes the podium. Reena *and Cruz turn their eyes toward her as she speaks into the microphone.*

"Inside this building, inscribed below our State Seal, are the words 'Senatoris est civitatis libertatem tueri,'" *Senator Gloria Fuller says to the crowd.* "This translates to: 'It is the duty of a senator to protect the liberty of the people.' That's exactly what I've been doing since my election to this position. And by the turnout here today, I'd like to think you feel that way, too."

The crowd erupts into applause. Cruz turns back to Reena.

"Extracurricular implies that you're going to school," *Cruz says with a smirk.* "I thought you dropped out."

She rolls her eyes. "Let me guess, you're a Harvard boy?"

Cruz shakes his head. "My brother, Simon, goes to Harvard. He's around here somewhere, too. But yeah, Yale was all like, 'Please, Cruz, we'll give you a full scholarship, we love you, we need you!' So, you know, how could I let them down?"

Reena laughs, amused by his cockiness. Just her type.

She motions to the neoclassical columns that line the Capitol building. "So, what? One day, you'll be in there with slicked hair and a suit to match?"

"Maybe," *he says.* "But I'm more concerned with where I'm taking you for dinner Saturday night."

"That might not be good for your squeaky-clean image."

"Then I guess we'll have to make sure it's worth it," *Cruz responds smoothly.*

Reena smiles. "Shouldn't you be helping my mom win or something?"

"Please. She's doing a fine job of that on her own."

Reena looks up, making eye contact with her mother. They don't always get along, but at the end of the day, they only really have each other.

And in that very moment, it's all ripped away.

A single gunshot rips through the air like a hammer. People scream, the crowd instinctively ducking. Then everything seems to slow down for Reena—her heart, her pulse, her view of things as they become distorted and surreal.

The police are running, scanning the crowd for the gunman, trying to figure out where the shot came from and who—if anyone—is hit. But Reena knows the target, isn't even surprised when she turns toward the podium to see her mother, a crumpled heap, on the ground. Blood seeps from a wound on her temple, fanning out in a crimson circle around her head.

A bloodcurdling scream echoes through the crowd. It takes Reena a moment to notice with detachment that it's hers.

Her mother's bodyguards appear at Reena's side as Cruz pushes through the crowd. She watches him stop, turn to his left, confusion and disbelief written all over his strong features. Reena follows his gaze to a group of policemen, surrounding a man who must be the shooter. One of the officers steps forward, pulling a wicked-looking shotgun from the man's body. As the other officers force the suspect to his feet, he begins shouting.

"Wait! This is a mistake! I didn't do it! I didn't do it!" The police cuff his hands behind his back as he continues to assert his innocence.

And then Reena's eyes find Cruz, frozen in place, staring

at the suspect as he's shoved through the crowd toward a battalion of police cars.

He says only one word, but even through the chaos, Reena hears it.

"Simon?"

REENA WAS STILL STEAMING OVER AVA'S WIN WHEN Cruz approached her. He could read her like a book. He knew she was pissed.

At him. At Takeda. At Ava.

But most of all at herself, for allowing Ava to beat her.

Pushing away the comforting hand Cruz tried to place on her shoulder, she turned her body away, Takeda's words still playing in her mind. But it was too late to show her independence. Takeda was watching, as always. The man missed nothing.

He shook his head, his disapproval evident.

"Sensei—" Reena began, wanting to redeem herself.

Takeda cut her short. "Revenge is a living organism. It thrives on focus, on discipline. While attempting to right your wrongs, many others will occur if you choose to lose that focus. You can only find and exploit your enemy's weaknesses if you shed your own." He pointed to her heart. "Start here."

He turned away, leaving her with Cruz.

"There will be other contests," he said gently, looking into her eyes. "Other opportunities to win."

"That doesn't change what happened with this one, does it?" she snapped, still bristling.

Cruz didn't flinch. He'd seen her at her worst. And this

was far from her worst. If she could have pushed him away, he would have been gone a long time ago. Romantic feelings aside, he was the only truly loyal person she had left. No matter what Takeda said, she was with Cruz for the long haul.

And they all had their baggage.

Ava stood with Takeda. Her eyes traveled to the mysterious young woman who rarely spoke, now practicing jujitsu in the rain. Whatever had happened to her, it must have been bad. And that was saying something in present company.

"What's her name?" Ava asked, eyes on the woman as she moved flawlessly from position to position.

"We call her Jane," Takeda said simply.

"What do you mean?" Ava asked. "That's not her real name?"

Takeda shot Ava a sharp look. "That is not for you to know, *deshi*."

Reena stifled a laugh at Takeda's use of the word for apprentice. Even Ava, it seemed, had to be put in her place from time to time.

Ava bowed her head, her cheeks pink. "I'm sorry, Sensei." She hesitated. "It's just . . ."

"Yes?" Takeda prompted.

"I was just wondering why she never participates in our drills."

Takeda seemed to consider the question. "I would not like anyone to become injured," he said as the winds picked up again.

"But she's been training for a while here, right?" Ava asked. "I'm sure she'd be okay."

Reena rolled her eyes. She really was clueless.

Takeda paused, as Jane's kicks turned lethal. She twisted her body around, slamming her fist into a thin Japanese pine tree, snapping it in two.

Takeda glanced meaningfully at Ava. "I was talking about the rest of you."

CHAPTER EIGHT

ORNING SUN STREAMED IN THROUGH THE atrium at Starling Vineyards, Chopin's Nocturne in C-sharp drifting like smoke through the halls of the house.

William Reinhardt's eyes were closed, his fingers moving expertly over the keys of the baby grand piano. He had just reached the crescendo when a ringing erupted from his pocket. He played a moment more, wanting to hold on to the music for just a few more seconds, before stopping with a sigh. He reached into his pocket and withdrew the phone, glancing at the display before accepting the call.

"Senator Wells, to what do I owe this pleasure?" Reinhardt asked.

"She found him," Jacob Wells said, a cacophony of echoing voices and footsteps on marble telling Reinhardt that he was probably in the California State Capitol building.

"Excellent." Reinhardt walked to the window, looking out over the rows of swollen Malbec and Nebbiolo grapes still glistening with dew. "Once again, she's proven herself an asset."

Wells's voice dropped a notch. "I still don't trust her."

Annoyance flared through Reinhardt's veins. He focused

on the grapes, forcing himself to speak evenly. "Just think of all she's done. And without asking anything in return."

"That's precisely what troubles me," the senator said.

"Everything is under control," Reinhardt said to pacify him. "This is the final piece of the puzzle. You'll be here for the Starling Gala on the first?"

"Of course." The senator didn't sound enthused.

"Good," Reinhardt said. "We'll exchange the information then."

He hung up the phone and walked back to the piano. Settling himself on the bench, he resumed Chopin's classic. He closed his eyes, letting the music move through him, return him to a time he'd tried without success to forget. It was always this way. First, the music: the only thing other than the vineyard that soothed his fury. But it never lasted long, because on the heels of the music came memories he did not want to face.

Rage built inside him, coating the inside of his mind with red paint until it was all he could see. Opening his eyes, he slammed his fist down onto the keys. The notes clanged eerily through the glass-enclosed room, sending the robins that made their home in the trees outside scurrying.

He stood, moving back to the open window. Taking a deep breath, he looked over the rows of vines, his gaze coming to rest on the other vineyards in the distance.

Reinhardt wanted it all. And he would stop at nothing to get it.

The ringing of his phone shook him out of his reverie. Probably that whiner Wells again. But when he looked at the display, he saw that it wasn't Wells but the woman Wells had phoned him about.

"I hear you found the missing link to my otherwise unbreakable chain," he said, approaching the minibar next to the baby grand for a morning cocktail. "I'd like to assume there's nothing you want, but I know human nature doesn't work that way."

"We'll get to that later." The voice on the other end of the phone was smooth, slightly husky. He always felt an oddly erotic thrill listening to her speak. "For now, I just want one thing."

Reinhardt poured himself a healthy glass of Cabernet, swirling it in the glass and holding it up to the light. "And what would that be?"

"For Starling Vineyards to remain in your possession."

CHAPTER NINE

"And as we lay her body to rest, we remember her gentle touch, her wistful laugh, her devoted heart. But most importantly we remember the one thing that won't be returned to the earth today. We remember the way Sylvie Anne Monroe made us feel. The way she still makes us feel. And unlike our physical bodies and even our mortal minds, that feeling is eternal. That feeling is forever."

The priest signals for the mahogany casket to begin its descent as tears stream down Ava's cheeks. The twenty-two-year-old mourner tries to keep her composure, to be as strong as Sylvie taught her, but it's hard.

A hand squeezes Ava's. It's firm and commanding, supportive and compassionate.

"You'll get through this, love," Charlie whispers in her ear, his breath breaking Ava from her grief-stricken trance.

"How?" she asks him.

He smiles. "Together."

They haven't known one another very long, barely a year, but Charlie and Ava's chemistry has fast-tracked their romance.

Even at a time when there's a hole in Ava's heart, Charlie fills it, mending it with his utter devotion.

A small bird flies past, causing both of them to jump. Ava laughs, looking at the bird wistfully.

"When the drunk driver killed my parents, Sylvie was with me every step of the way." She looked up at him. "Just like you are now."

"What does that have to do with the bird?" Charlie asks, puzzled.

Ava bends down, picks up a handful of sought-after Napa dirt, and lets it slide through her fingers.

"After my great-grandfather died, Sylvie decided to take the land she inherited from him and start a winery. He had purchased the land in the mid-1960s, before Napa became known for its wine. It wasn't long before it became a big deal. But the winery needed a name. Something compelling, something that felt right for my mother and grandmother, both overcoming the passing of a patriarch by doing something audacious and daunting." She smiled. "It turned out my mother's favorite bird was the starling, a winged warrior that can survive almost anywhere, from the glaciers of the Arctic to the tropical forests surrounding the equator. And everywhere in between."

Charlie reaches into his pocket and removes the small, novelty cork key chain Ava gave him the first time they met.

Ava stands, wiping the treasured dirt off her hands. She catches Charlie looking at her with a gentle smile.

"Starlings," she finishes, "have the ability to endure. To persist. And most importantly, to adapt."

THE MOON WAS JUST A SLIVER, SHINING FAINT LIGHT ON the sea below. Ava and Jon sat side by side on the rocky ledge, gazing out over the water in companionable silence. She didn't know when their midnight meetings had become part of her routine, but at some point, she'd come to expect him there, waiting on the edge of the cliff when she couldn't sleep.

There was chemistry, although she could never be sure Jon felt it, too. But this wasn't the time or the place for a romantic entanglement. She was beginning to see that the path ahead would be almost as difficult as the one she'd already traveled. A relationship would only make things more complicated. Plus, Jon was turning into a friend. Maybe even a good one.

And those were in very short supply at the moment.

Besides, she didn't even know if Jon was attracted to her. Sometimes she thought she saw it. She would glance up to see him turn away, like he'd been caught looking at her. Or he would hold her hand just a little longer than necessary as he helped her up from getting her ass kicked by Reena or Cruz. But a moment later, it would be gone, Jon's face as guarded as ever.

"Are you ever going to tell me what happened to you?" he asked.

The question surprised her. They had never spoken about their pasts. Had never even asked the question. She'd assumed that was how he wanted it.

"Are you?" she asked, hedging.

He chuckled.

"What?"

"Just . . . you," he said smiling, his brown eyes warm. "You keep me on my toes."

She laughed. "Only because Reena keeps me on mine."

Their rivalry had become legendary. Ava sometimes wondered if Reena would throw her over the cliff into the channel if given the opportunity.

"Whatever the reason, I like it," he said.

"Yeah?"

He nodded, a slow smile emerging on his full lips. "Yeah." They sat a minute more before he spoke again. "So are you?"

She punched him playfully in the arm. "You're relentless."

"You're one to talk."

For a minute, all she could do was watch the water, listen to the ebb and flow of the waves, bringing her memories home. She'd worked to keep them at bay. Calling them forward took effort.

"His name was Charlie," she began. After that, it was easier than she expected. She told Jon everything. The death of her parents and her subsequent life with her grandmother. The vineyard, learning every row of fruit, every field of flowers, every oak barrel until the wine they bottled was as much a part of her as the blood flowing through her veins.

A reminder of her parents and the legacy that was Ava's.

And then, her grandmother's death. Charlie. William Reinhardt. The loss of everything.

By the time she was finished, she felt like her heart was in a vise. There were no tears. She'd used those up a long time ago. But the despair was still there, the desolation lurking in the corners of her heart, seeping forward like sludge.

Jon surprised her by taking her hand. His skin was warm and dry.

"I'm sorry," he said softly. "Bastards."

She took a deep breath, nodding. "Yeah."

"You'll make them pay. Put things back in balance."

She looked over at him, their eyes meeting. Her thigh, bare under her robe, brushed against his sweatpant-clad leg, sending a ripple of electricity all the way into her chest.

"Yes."

He squeezed her hand.

"What about you?" she asked carefully.

They were all wounded, broken, angry. Ava, Reena, Cruz, even the young woman they called Jane. Ava was known for her determination. Reena for her rage. Cruz for his desire to protect Reena. And Jane for her deadly force.

But Jon remained a mystery. Closed off and distant, Jon seemed only to connect with Ava. Still, she was surprised when he started talking.

"Her name was Courtney," he said quietly. "The love of my life. We were going to be married."

Ava was stunned, both by the revelation that he had been engaged and by the unfamiliar sting of jealousy that accompanied it. She squeezed his hand, forcing her voice steady.

"Tell me."

"I found her lying lifeless in the street, in Sonoma, where we lived."

Ava's surprise that Jon lived near her hometown of Napa was blunted by the pain evident in his voice.

"What happened?"

He shook his head, his broad shoulders tensing under the thin T-shirt he wore at night. "It's a long story, but the people responsible never paid for what they did to her."

"I'm so sorry," Ava said softly.

She could feel him retreating, backing away from her,

going someplace dark. She knew the place well. Was intimately familiar with its bleakness, with all the dangerous things that lurked in its shadows.

"I know who did it," Jon continued. "I just can't get close enough to them to make them pay."

She turned toward him and looked into his eyes. It was important that he believed he would get justice for those who couldn't get it for themselves. For the woman he loved. Believing was the only thing that kept them going. The only thing that would keep them going in the days and weeks ahead.

"You will," she said firmly. "We all will."

Time seemed to stop. There were only inches between them, Jon's face so close to hers she could smell the mint on his breath. He reached out for her arms, caressing them over her robe, sending a rush of exquisite desire through her body.

It was a bad idea. For more than one reason, revenge being the first and most important. But that was her head talking. Her heart and body seemed to have other ideas as Jon pulled a strand of windblown hair from her face, his fingers brushing her cheek.

"Ava . . . ," he started.

She placed her fingers against his lips. She didn't want him to say it, whatever it was.

He took her hand, opening her fingers and placing a gentle kiss in her palm. And then he was leaning in, lowering his mouth to hers just before something smashed into them, sending them crashing brutally to the ground near the cliff's edge.

CHAPTER TEN

THEIR TRAINING HAD BEEN MORE EFFECTIVE THAN Ava realized. It only took her a moment to switch gears, the kiss forgotten as she tried to get to her feet and assess the situation.

But she didn't have time. She was only halfway to standing when something came at her from the shadows, pinning her to the ground with beastly strength. A face loomed above her, but the darkness made it difficult to make out any features.

Besides, Ava had bigger problems. Like the fact that her head was dangling over the edge of the cliff, her attacker holding an arm to her throat, cutting off her air supply.

She forced her mind calm. Forced herself to catalog her options, few though they were.

Her vision was growing black around the edges, unconsciousness beckoning, when she finally grasped at an idea. Thrashing her lower body, she tried to shimmy the attacker off her legs and hips until she could lift her knees. It worked. Focused on her neck, the assaulter leaned into her chest, instinctively avoiding the resistance of her lower body.

She couldn't see Jon, didn't know what had happened to

him. Could there have been more than one attacker? She didn't know, but this might be the only chance she would get to escape and possibly to help Jon, too.

Wishing she had more room to maneuver, she rocked her lower body until she had just enough momentum to spring to her feet, the movement knocking her assailant off balance, giving Ava a welcome break from the onslaught. Ava caught sight of Jon getting to his feet near the cliff's edge, landing a punch to the assaulter's face that hardly seemed to diminish the severity of the aggression.

Ava didn't know how long the two traded punches and kicks before Jon landed two harsh blows to the attacker's head. Ava was just about to breathe a sigh of relief when the aggressor came rocketing from the ground, pummeling Jon with a ferocious kick to the chest. Jon stumbled backward, shock seeping across his face.

"Jane, no!" Reena shouted, running toward them.

Jane? Ava looked wildly around, trying to figure out what was going on.

But yes, the attacker was Jane, still in her nightgown, blinking at Reena like she didn't quite recognize her as Jon clutched at his chest and their attacker tried to stand.

Reena grabbed ahold of Jane's arm, shoving her toward Cruz, who immediately locked her arms behind her back.

"Stop it!" he shouted as she fought him, trying to get away.

For a few seconds, Ava thought it was over, but then Jane snapped her arms free, flipping Cruz effortlessly over her shoulder. He landed on his back with a dull thud and lay there, looking up at her with a mixture of anger and admiration.

"You're going to have to teach me how to do that," he croaked.

Ava shook her head. "Why is she attacking us?" she shouted.

"Grab her legs!" Reena instructed, ignoring Ava's question.

Jane was moving in circles, surveying them like a feral animal calculating its escape. Ava maintained eye contact with Reena, who clearly knew more about what was going on than Ava did.

"You saw what she did to Cruz?" Reena shouted to Ava.

She nodded her understanding, and the two moved in unison. Reena quickly grabbed for Jane's left ankle while Ava took the right. Working in sync, they flipped Jane over their shoulders, sending her crashing to the ground.

Finally, everyone was still. Jon and Cruz stood off to one side, eyeing Jane with caution, while Reena and Ava gasped for breath.

Jane lay there for a minute, her chest rising and falling as her eyes slowly cleared. Finally she groaned, looking up at them.

"Oh my God," she said. "I did it again, didn't I?"

CHAPTER ELEVEN

I T WAS THE FIRST TIME AVA HAD HEARD JANE SPEAK.
Her voice was sweeter than Ava expected after weeks of
watching her move through Takeda's deadly exercises.

"Again?" Ava asked.

"Jane has nightmares," Cruz explained, coming toward
them. "Sometimes they turn—"

"Violent," Jane finished, getting to her feet.

Ava glanced at her, still wary. But Jane seemed lucid and
clear-eyed. The wound on her face had opened up, a thin
trickle of blood running down the fine bone of her cheek, but
she either didn't notice or didn't care.

Jon rubbed his neck. "Well, I guess you know our names."

Jane nodded. "I'm sorry I haven't spoken. I've been . . ."
She shook her head. "I've been in a bad place. Trying to re-
cover, regroup, figure things out."

"We all understand needing to do those things," Reena said.

But Ava was still getting her head around what had happened. Still reeling from the fact that mild-mannered Jane
had attacked them with a vengeance.

"What happened to you?" she asked.

Jane took a deep breath. "I don't know. A little over a year ago I woke up here, on Rebun Island. I didn't know my name, where I came from . . . I couldn't have told you what I looked like without looking in a mirror." She chuckled sadly. "I still don't recognize myself."

Shocked, Ava reached a hand toward Jane's face. "That cut . . ."

Jane touched a finger tenderly to her cheek, her fingers coming away smeared with blood. "I don't even remember where it came from."

Reena removed the belt from her robe and stepped toward Jane. "May I?"

Jane shook her head. "I don't want you to ruin your robe."

"Don't be ridiculous," Reena said, touching the folded-up piece of cloth to Jane's face.

Jane winced.

"I'm sorry," Reena said. "Just hold that there until it stops bleeding."

Ava tried not to stare. Was this Reena being *nice*?

"Can't Takeda explain what happened to you?" Jon asked. "He must know if you ended up at the tera."

It wasn't Jane who answered but Cruz.

"He's the only one who knows, but he thinks it's best for Jane to remember on her own, that when she does get her memory back, she's going to be glad she's here training."

"But if he knows who you are and what happened to you, why does he call you Jane?" Ava asked.

"Forcing her to confront her memories—even something

simple like her name—before her psyche is ready could cause her trauma. Or at least that's what Takeda says," Reena explained.

Ava wondered if she was imagining the note of skepticism in Reena's voice.

"When I do remember," Jane said, "Takeda is sure I'll want revenge."

"Which is why you're here, preparing with the rest of us."

She nodded, moving the fabric from her cut and checking to see if it was still bleeding.

"She's like a goddamn weapon," Cruz said. "I could've used her back in high school during 'stuff Cruz in the locker' day. Which was basically every day."

He started to laugh, but Reena shot him a withering glance that shut him up fast. Wrong place, wrong time.

"I'm so sorry," Jane said. "My nightmares . . . I usually don't remember them," she said softly.

Ava stepped toward her. "But you did this time?"

Jane looked up at her, tawny eyes full of confusion. "Not much. Just . . . a car, coming toward me. Coming too fast. And I think . . ."

"What is it?" Ava prompted.

"I think I recognized the person behind the wheel, but now I can't remember the face."

"That doesn't sound like a dream," Jon said.

"Then what is it?" Jane asked.

"Sounds like a memory to me."

They were standing in silence, Jon's words swirling around them with the wind from the channel, when the sound of shattering porcelain broke through the night. They turned toward the tera, glancing quickly at each other before taking off at a run.

They raced toward the temple, moving past their sleeping quarters and maneuvering around the elaborate maze and fencing turf where they had spent countless hours training. They had just rounded the corner of the temple when Ava spotted a tall man in a ski mask, dressed in army fatigues and holding a burlap sack, outside the meditation room.

She pointed. "Over there!"

They turned their attention to the intruder, a sturdy Japanese torii gate blocking his escape on one side, a small shed blocking it on the other.

Taking advantage of the man's momentary indecision, Reena rushed forward, lunging at him. He ducked, somersaulting under her while keeping his grip on the sack, sending Reena sprawling atop the broken pieces of the Buddha deity Acala, which had once sat on an altar under the window.

Ava and the others closed in on the thief as he backed toward the dried-out fire pit in front of the torii gate. Takeda's dogs, a beautiful pack of blue-eyed Akitas, barked and howled in the distance, agitated by the commotion.

"You made a mistake," Reena snarled, on her feet again and moving forward with the others.

Ava felt a flash of admiration. Reena didn't seem the least bit fazed by anything that had happened.

They circled the intruder, each of them moving in, closing the distance as Takeda had taught them. Indecision played on the man's face as he considered his options. A moment later, he threw the bag to the ground.

Taking it as a concession, Ava bent down to pick it up. But

the intruder wasn't done. He used the distraction to rush past her, gunning for the corner of the tera in an attempt to get clear of them. Cruz and Jon took off after him, bringing him down just as he reached the old shed.

Jon pinned him to the ground, holding him there while Cruz tore off his mask. Ava was surprised to see that he was older, maybe even middle-aged. He shouted something in Japanese. As they looked at each other, trying to figure out how to handle the language barrier, Jane spoke.

"He wants you to let him go."

They all turned to her in surprise.

Cruz shook his head, refocusing on the bandit, still immobilized by Jon. "Well, that's not happening."

The man continued to shout in Japanese as he tried to squirm free of Jon's grip.

"He says if you let him go he'll never return," Jane said. "He's sorry."

Ava couldn't hide her surprise. She knew linguistics was supposed to be part of their training, but they hadn't yet gotten to that part. Clearly, Jane was way ahead of them.

"Takeda wants us to speak many languages," Jane explained. "To have many guises. You'll see."

"I only know one Japanese word," Ava said.

"Which one?" Jane asked.

She was preparing to answer when she spotted Takeda, making his way toward them from the tera.

He stepped over the fire pit, looking at the captured intruder before turning his gaze on his students.

"Well? What do you propose we do to him, *deshis?*"

CHAPTER TWELVE

THEY SURVEYED THE BANDIT, SITTING ON A WOODEN
stool below the large open window inside the meditation
room. He shivered, candlelight flickering eerily across his face.

"Let's try this again," said Cruz. "Who are you? Why are
you here?"

The thief shook his head, a move he'd made countless times
in the thirty minutes they'd been interrogating him. So far,
they'd gotten nothing out of him. The sack he'd been carrying had been filled with the burlap bags Takeda had given
them when they first arrived on Rebun Island—bags that had
been tucked away so they could focus on the path to revenge
instead of the pasts that had brought them here.

"Let's throw him to the dogs," Reena suggested, voice
hard as she motioned toward the outdoor pen where the
Akitas were still barking.

"Don't worry." Sarcasm was thick in Cruz's voice. "She
doesn't mean that."

"Yes, I do," Reena said.

Cruz glanced over at her before returning his gaze to
the thief. "Okay, maybe she does."

Takeda spoke for the first time since they'd brought the man inside. "Cruz," he said, "what should we do with him?"

Cruz seemed to think about it. "I suppose the dogs do sound hungry," he finally said.

Takeda's face was impassive.

Jon stepped forward. "I say we take what he has. An eye for an eye, right?"

"Wait!" Jane pleaded. "Don't you think we should know his story first?"

"We tried that," Cruz answered. "The guy won't talk."

Takeda looked at Ava. "Do you not have an opinion?"

Ava did, but she was still trying to figure out if it was based on evidence or her lack of sleep.

"I think we should let him go," she finally said.

Everyone grew quiet as they turned to stare at her. Then the room erupted into chaos, each of them giving their own reasons why they thought Ava was crazy.

"Wait." Takeda's voice cut through the noise. He nodded at Ava. "Continue."

"The thing is," Ava began, "he only took our personal items. Pictures, old letters, mementos from our past . . . Why would he bother? Plus, he shouldn't even know where the satchels are hidden." She paused, turning to the wall of the meditation room and removing a panel, revealing a hole where the satchels had been stored. She looked at Takeda. "Only we know that, and only because we were with you when you stored them away."

"Go on," Takeda said.

"Well, look at the timing. He broke in forty minutes ago, when we were all awake and outside, easily able to hear any noise he might make."

Takeda raised one eyebrow. "So?"

Ava took a deep breath. "So he's not a thief."

The room erupted again into protests.

"Look at him," Ava said, nodding to the man sitting calmly on the wooden stool. "The window's wide open. If he thought he was in danger, why didn't he just jump out the window? I mean, if he can break in, it seems to me he could probably break out. It's not like we tied him up or anything." Ava continued, more sure of herself now that she'd said it all out loud. "He's not a thief. He's a test. Hired by Takeda to see how we would handle the situation. To see what kind of justice—or mercy—we would exact on him."

The room was silent as everyone took in Ava's words. Reena's expression was tight, her face a mask of barely contained anger.

Takeda simply nodded. "You have exceeded my expectations."

Ava bowed. "Thank you, Sensei."

Takeda walked over to the man on the stool, patted his back, and spoke to him in Japanese. The man chuckled and stood, turning for the door.

"You may all retire for the evening," Takeda said. He picked the satchel up off the floor and handed it to Jon. "Please, secure this in its proper place."

Jon bowed. "Yes, Sensei."

The others left, crunching across the broken statue outside the meditation room. Stepping outside, Ava kneeled on the gravel, picking up the porcelain shards.

"Some things cannot be fixed," Takeda said, stopping at her side. "We can only let them go."

"But it was so beautiful," Ava said, an irrational burst of sadness rising in her chest. She had walked past the statue a hundred times and never even noticed it.

Takeda bent next to her, picking up one of the jagged fragments. He studied it before speaking again.

"Objects are of little value. It is the lessons I impart that will prove long-lasting."

Ava looked at the face of the statue, still intact, her green eyes reflected in the angry, expressive face engulfed in flames. "What does it mean?"

"Acala is said to protect all the living."

"Why is he on fire?" Ava asked, trying to fit two of the broken pieces together.

"It is said that burning away all weaknesses is the only way to find truth. To achieve enlightenment." Takeda stood. "Good night, Ava."

He left on silent feet, swallowed by the night only seconds later.

Ava rose, wanting to clean up the broken porcelain before she went to bed. She was turning to go when she noticed a small fragment of Acala's flame on the ground near her feet. She picked it up, the porcelain glimmering in what was left of the moonlight.

She tucked the piece into her palm and went to look for a broom.

CHAPTER THIRTEEN

AVA LET THE BROKEN PIECES SLIDE FROM THE dustpan into the waste bin. Then she put the broom away and went inside. Jon was still there, tightening the panel onto the wall. He looked over his shoulder at her.

"Hey," he said, turning back to the panel.

"Hey. How's it going?"

"I think I've just . . . about . . . got it." He gave the panel one last shimmy. A solid click sounded through the room. "There." He turned to her. "I'm surprised you're still up."

"I wanted to clean up the mess outside before I went to bed."

He nodded, his eyes lingering on her face. Ava was suddenly aware of their solitude in the meditation room. Everyone else had gone to bed, the tera and its residents finally settled down for the night. The waves crashed against the cliffs below, a rhythmic lullaby that was the only sound in the still night.

She had a flash of his lips, warm and insistent against hers, before they'd been interrupted on the cliff. And here they were again, just inches apart, like the universe was conspiring to throw them together in spite of the danger.

And there *was* danger. Of losing focus. Of opening her

heart to someone who was still grieving the loss of his dead fiancée. Of opening her heart to anyone, for that matter.

She tried to calm the rush of desire in her veins. "I guess we should go to bed."

He held her gaze a moment longer before turning reluctantly away. "I guess so."

Ava was halfway to the door when she heard Jon's voice behind her.

"What the . . . ?"

Turning around, she saw Jon studying something against the wall. She walked over and leaned in, her eyes finding a tiny crack in the rice paper paneling of the meditation room wall.

"What is it?" Ava asked.

Jon reached out, pushing gently against the wall until a huge rectangle seemed to open up in front of them, the panel swinging inward.

A hidden door.

Jon grabbed a candle from a nearby altar and stepped toward the dark recesses of the room beyond.

Ava put a hand on his arm. "Do you think we should?"

He turned to her, indecision in his eyes. "You probably shouldn't. I don't want you to get in trouble. But I'm going to see what's in here."

Ava sighed and followed him in.

The room was so dark she couldn't see anything beyond the small circle of light cast by the candle. She grabbed on to Jon's arm, giving her eyes time to adjust to the blackness around her. It didn't help much, but a few seconds later, Jon extended his arm, holding the candle out in front of him and moving it around until Ava could make out the contents of the room.

It was tiny, not much bigger than a closet. There was a small writing desk against one wall, a simple stool, and an un-lit candle, burned halfway down. There were no pictures on the wall, no personal effects to hint at the room's purpose or owner, although Ava had to guess it was Takeda.

Jon stepped toward the desk, a stack of files sitting neatly atop its surface. Setting the candle down, he picked them up, opening the one on top.

"Jon . . ."

He ignored her, setting the file down and opening the next one. And the next and the next.

"These are ours," he muttered.

"What are ours?" Ava asked.

"The files." He picked up the first one from the desk. "This is mine. Information on the people who destroyed my life."

Jon handed her the folder. She flipped through the con-tents, past schedules, calendars, receipts, and repeated men-tions of a man named Frederick Cain.

Ava closed the file. "Is mine in there?"

He met her eyes in the flickering light of the candle.

She held out her hand. "Let me see."

He hesitated before turning back to the stack of files, riffling through them until he got to the one he was looking for. He handed it to her.

She knew the folder was hers, but somehow she was still surprised to see her name scrawled in black marker across the top left corner. It felt like a violation. An intrusion on the past that belonged only to her.

But that was stupid. That Takeda knew about her past had never been a question.

She bent her head to the papers inside the file, immediately transported back to Starling Vineyards. Napa. Home.

There were documents detailing Ava's family history, land surveys of the vineyard, copies of deeds old and new, even Ava's college transcript. Most importantly, there was information on the people who had taken it all away.

She came to the end of the file, her eyes falling on a black-and-white photograph of Charles Bay, smiling into the camera. Even now, it was like a punch to the stomach, one that brought memories she wasn't at all prepared to face.

Ava and Charlie walk hand in hand across the cobblestone streets of St. Helena, a modest diamond glittering on Ava's finger. The sun is shining, the air warm and arid in a way unique to Napa and Sonoma counties. Ava shields her eyes against the sun, and Charlie stops to remove a pair of sunglasses from the outdoor display of a small boutique.

He puts the glasses gently on her face. "Perfection."

Ava laughs, but Charlie takes a twenty-dollar bill from his pocket and hands it to the store owner, an older gentleman with a receding hairline and growing waistline.

"Can't let the lady suffer," Charlie says, winking at him.

Charlie puts his arm around her and they continue walking.

"You didn't have to do that," she says.

"What, the sunglasses? Ava, it's okay, I want you to——"

She stops walking, forcing him to stop, too, and pulls him out of the walkway. "You don't owe me anything. This is something I want to do. For us. So no more thank-yous, no more gifts, no more——"

Charlie leans in, kissing her.

"Well, okay, you can keep doing that," she says, still surprised by the effect he has on her. They laugh. She looks up at him as they continue walking. "We're in this together, right? Forever?"

He nods slowly. "I just want you to be sure."

They finally come to a stop in front of a small office, an old wooden sign swinging from the façade: LAW OFFICE OF MEYER HERMAN & DUNN, ESQUIRE.

She looks into his eyes. "What about you? Are you sure?"

He squeezes her hand. "I've never been more sure of anything in my entire life."

She smiles. "Me, too. The land, the winery, my home—our home—it's all I have left of them. My parents. Grandma Sylvie. I want to share it with someone. With you."

He leans in, kissing her tenderly. "I love you, Ava, and purchasing that land in the Loire Valley will be an incredible way to expand the winery—and your family's legacy."

"Are you sure I can't see the land first?" she asks. "I'd really love to."

Charlie sighs, shaking his head. "I know, love. But we talked about this. The season is kicking into high gear around here. I thought you couldn't get away?"

"Well, yes, not right now," Ava says. "But in a few months—"

"In a few months it will be gone. It's such a rarity for a property like this one to come on the market. And at least I was able to see it when I was last in France." He pauses. "Maybe we should take our chances. I don't want you to be uncomfortable with the idea."

But *Ava doesn't want to lose the property. Doesn't want to disappoint Charlie when he's worked so hard to help her with the vineyard, when he's put so much faith into their future.*

"And once the deal goes through . . ."

"Just like we talked about," he says excitedly. "You're only granting me power of attorney so I can sign the deeds to the Loire Valley. When the deal is done, we'll put everything back in your name."

It's time to move on. Time to put the sadness and loss of the past aside for a joyful future with Charlie.

She takes a deep breath. "Okay, then. Let's do it."

Charlie crushes her in a quick embrace before opening the door to the law office and ushering her inside.

——————————

CHAPTER FOURTEEN

"WHY WOULD TAKEDA KEEP THIS STUFF FROM US?" Jon said, leaning against the wall.

Reena was sitting on the floor next to Cruz, each of them paging through their files. She'd assumed Takeda knew things about her, about the death of her mother, but she'd been shocked silent by the breadth of his knowledge. Even she, someone who rarely apologized for herself or her behavior, was embarrassed by the revelations. The drunkenness, the partying, the sleeping around . . . Everything that had come before her mother's murder.

"Maybe part of revenge is learning about our enemies so we can take them down the right way," Ava suggested, sitting at the old wooden table that functioned as a desk in her room.

Jon paced. "These files have everything I need to track and confront Cain. What's the point in waiting?"

"Takeda has a reason for everything," Ava said. "If he hasn't shown us these files, it's because he doesn't think we're ready."

Reena was only half listening, her eyes drawn to a photograph of a middle-aged man with piercing eyes. "Cruz, look at this."

He reached for the photo. "Is that Senator Wells?"

Reena swallowed, trying to quell the dread creeping through her bones. "I think so."

"Wait a minute," Ava said. "Isn't Senator Wells the guy who took over after—"

"After my mother was killed?" Reena said softly. "Yes."

"You always said you never trusted the guy," Cruz murmured. "And don't you remember that paper of his you found? The one with the—"

"I remember it," Reena snapped, her heart in a vise. "What's your point?"

"Take a look." He handed her a stack of grainy photographs from his own file.

"What is this?" Reena asked, looking down at the images. Her gaze was drawn to a man with glasses. He looked more like a computer programmer than someone who belonged in the world of murder for hire. "*Who* is it?"

Crossing the room, Jon leaned over Reena's shoulder to look at the pictures. "They look like security camera screen shots." He froze, eyes glued to the photos. "What the fuck?"

Reena glanced at Jon. "What is it?"

He pointed to the man meeting with Wells. "That's Frederick Cain." He looked at Reena. "You said they never found the person who killed your mother?"

She nodded, despair encroaching on the serenity she'd found focusing on revenge. "Cruz's brother, Simon, was arrested and found guilty, but there's no way he did it."

Jon stood, running his hand through his hair. "This is crazy."

"What's going on?" Ava asked.

"Frederick Cain is a hit man," he said, turning to them. "Actually, that's not totally true. He hires people to do the dirty work. But he's the guy you call when you want to take someone out and don't want to do it yourself."

"How do you know all of this?" Reena asked, her mind working to put the pieces together.

"Because Cain and his people are the ones who killed my fiancée."

Reena stood up, wanting to crawl out of her own skin as everything began to fall into place. If Wells had Cain kill her mother and framed Cruz's brother—a safe assumption given the photos of them meeting in Cruz's revenge file—and Cain also killed Jon's fiancée . . .

Their missions were connected. They were out for revenge against the same people.

"According to these printouts—hacked government files, police reports—Cain is exactly who Jon says he is," Cruz said, looking at the contents of the file. "But no one's ever been able to nail the dude. Hell, no one's even connected him with a crime. Ever."

"Cain has friends in high places," Jon explained. "And everyone has a price. He orchestrates everything and then pays off the right people to keep it all quiet. Convenient, since most of the people he's paying off are the same ones paying him to commit their own personal sins."

Reena's despair receded, transforming into the cold fury she'd relied on since coming to Rebun Island. Now it all made sense; Senator Wells hired Cain to kill Reena's mother so he could take her seat in the Senate.

"This is weird," Cruz muttered, picking up the files and consulting them one by one. "Every one of our files has a calendar page with May first circled and marked with '10 p.m., Starling Vineyards, Napa Valley.'"

Ava froze, shaking her head. "What did you just say?"

Cruz handed her the files. "See for yourself."

Ava flipped through the folders before sinking onto a chair, her face a mask of shock.

"That mean something to you?" Cruz asked.

"Starling Vineyards is mine. Was mine." She looked up at them. "It was in my family for three generations before it was taken from me. Every year on May first a gala is held there."

"What kind of gala?" Reena asked.

"It's a formal event: wine, food, dancing, the whole nine yards," Ava explained. "My grandmother started the tradition. After she passed, I upheld it. Apparently the bastards who stole my life have kept it going."

"May first is next week and it looks like both Senator Wells and Frederick Cain will be there," Jon said.

But there was something Reena didn't understand. "Why are they meeting at some château in Northern California?"

Ava looked away, her mind coming to some unpleasant conclusions.

"Do you know something we don't?" Reena asked her.

Ava sighed. "I'm guessing it's because of William Reinhardt."

"Who's William Reinhardt?" Jon asked.

Ava opened her file and removed a picture of an elegant

man with salt-and-pepper hair and a thinly groomed beard. "This man."

Reena had never seen the man before in her life. "What does he have to do with anything?"

"Well, I'm assuming a senator wouldn't be well acquainted with hit men," Ava said. "If Jacob Wells wanted someone to take out your mother, he'd need a connection to find that kind of someone."

"And this guy, Reinhardt, is that connection?" Cruz asked.

Ava shrugged. "Who knows? But it makes sense. He's a big-money investor who uses questionable tactics to get what he wants. It's made him a very wealthy man, and according to Takeda's files, he and Senator Wells were roommates at Brown. Plus, Reinhardt's been rumored to have associations with Cain, using him and his men to intimidate, and sometimes worse, to get what he wants."

"And to get his friends what they want," Reena said angrily. "Even if it was murdering my mother."

Reena storms into a seedy motel room, bare and grimy, made up of two wiry twin beds and a termite-infested desk. Cruz follows Reena inside, shutting the door and locking it behind her.

"The media won't give us two seconds together. Won't give me two seconds to myself," Cruz says, pacing the tiny room.

"This place is disgusting," Reena says, looking around.

"Yeah, well, at least they won't find us here."

"I wouldn't even be able to find us here," Reena says.

Cruz crosses his muscular arms across his chest. "Funny. I haven't been able to find you for the last six months."

Reena looked down, guilt crowding out her happiness at seeing Cruz. The shooting of Reena's mother and Simon's subsequent arrest had sent both their lives into a tailspin. At first, they had banded together, finding solace in each other's company, and eventually, each other's arms. But then Simon's trial had begun, and Reena's life had turned into a media feeding frenzy. Overwhelmed and distraught, Reena had done the only thing she could at the time. She'd run.

Reena grabs Cruz's hand and pulls him next to her on the edge of one of the beds. "I'm sorry. I'm going to explain, I promise. But first, tell me about Simon. How is he holding up?"

Cruz stares at her a minute, as if trying to determine if he can really trust her to come clean.

Finally, he shakes his head. "He's hanging in there, but I think he's starting to crack. We used to think we could get him out on appeal, but the lawyers say that's probably not going to happen unless we can introduce some kind of new evidence. I just . . ."

Reena tips her head, forcing him to look at her. "What?"

"I just feel so fucking helpless."

"I'm sorry," she says softly, wrapping her arms around him. She knows that the brothers hadn't had an easy childhood. But they had each other, and that had gotten them through the hard times. It must be killing Cruz not to be able to help Simon.

"Is the press still speculating that you were in on it?" Reena had been shocked and horrified when the media had gone after Cruz, insinuating that, as an aide to Reena's mother, he had fed Simon information that allowed him to get close enough to take the shot that had killed her.

He waved off the question. "I'm done in politics. Ruined. But I don't even care anymore. I just need to clear Simon."

"Have you found out anything new?" Reena asks. "Anything that might help?"

He shakes his head. "I've hit so many brick walls, my head is bleeding. I'm at a dead end."

She hesitates. He's as stubborn as she is. Once she tells him her plan, there will be no going back. For either of them.

"I think I might be able to help," she finally says.

"Have you found something? Some kind of new evidence?"

She takes a deep breath. "I found someone," she says. "Someone who can help us clear Simon's name. Someone who can help us find my mother's killer. Who can teach us how to avenge them both."

"Avenge?" Cruz shakes his head. "What are you talking about?"

Reena stands up. There's only one way to make Cruz understand. Only one way to make him see.

She walks calmly over to the bedside table, smashing her fist into the lamp on its surface. Shards of ceramic fly through the air before falling to the dilapidated carpet at their feet.

Cruz stands, a look of shock on his face. "What the fuck was that?"

Reena picks up a piece of the demolished lamp. "He'll show us everything we need to know," she says, launching the ceramic shard like an arrow at a dingy clock hanging on the wall.

It hits the target square in the center. Bull's-eye.

Cruz stares at her like he's never seen her before. "Everything we need to know for what?"

Reena meets his eyes. "Revenge."

CHAPTER FIFTEEN

THE GROUP HAD BEEN SILENT, EACH OF THEM TRY-
ing to process everything they'd learned from their files,
when Reena finally looked up at Ava.

"I see the connection between Wells, Cain, Reinhardt,
and the rest of us, but what do they have to do with you? How
are you connected to all this?"

"The man who took my family's land was my husband,"
Ava said. "Well, I thought he was my husband. But he didn't
do it alone."

Reena raised her eyebrows. "Reinhardt?"

"The one and only," Ava confirmed.

"He got someone to marry you to take your land?" Jon
asked.

Ava was surprised to find that she was no longer embarrassed by the admission. No longer angry at her naïveté. No
longer angry at all. The fury that had consumed her had been
replaced by something cold and calculating. A beast that demanded not vengeance, but justice, just as Takeda said.

"There's not much room for expansion in Napa," Ava
explained. "The existing vineyards are old and family-run.

There's no way they would sell, especially not to someone like Reinhardt who was all about profit, who didn't understand the real value of the land and the responsibility of that legacy. My parents had died, my grandmother..." She shrugged. "I was alone. And Charlie, Reinhardt's lackey, was very, very good."

Cruz nodded his understanding. "Those kinds of people are all the same. They have no respect for anything."

"Exactly," Ava said. "And Reinhardt didn't just ruin me and my legacy. From what I hear, he's introducing his brand of intimidation and coercion to the other vintners in an attempt to increase his stake." She called up a fresh round of determination. "I let him in. It's my job to set things straight."

"Well, I guess now we know why Takeda's been training us together," Cruz said.

Jon throws his file onto the desk. "I'm done with Takeda's training. I'm going after Cain and everyone who works for him."

"You can't do that," Ava protested. "Not yet. 'Death by a thousand cuts,' remember? We have to be smart."

Reena walked over to Ava. "If we can expose these sons of bitches, they will all go down. Including your former boy-toy. I thought you wanted vengeance."

"I do. I just think we should talk to Takeda before we do anything rash."

"He'll only try to stop us," Jon said.

"Which is exactly why we should give him a chance to explain. To advise," Ava said. "He's taught us so much already. We have to trust that he knows what he's doing."

Jon looked at her. "Seems to me that trusting people is what got you here in the first place."

"You don't need to remind me of that," she snapped. "Not a day goes by that I don't remember."

He held her eyes, a different kind of spark running between them as she fumed.

Finally, he sighed, walking over to her. "I'm sorry. I shouldn't have said that. But we don't have much time before May first and I think we should do something." He surprised her by putting his hands on either side of her face. He looked deeply into her eyes. "You deserve to breathe easy, Ava. We all do."

"Agreed," Cruz said.

Ava folded her arms across her chest. She was outnumbered. If they were determined to go, what could she do but go with them? It seemed they were in it together now.

Reena's expression softened. "Listen, I get where you're coming from. We all want to do the right thing here. The best thing. But we've lost so much, Ava. It's time to do something about it."

"Not without me you won't."

They turned to see Jane standing in the doorway, already dressed in black.

"How long have you been there?" Cruz asked.

"Long enough to know that if what you said is true, I'm connected to your mission, too. Which means one of the men you've been talking about is responsible for what happened to me."

"We can't be sure of that," Ava protested. She stood up and gazed at the large antique mirror hanging above the desk. "For all we know there's another player we haven't been introduced to yet."

"It doesn't matter," Jane said, stepping farther into the

room. "I've been in the dark too long. This is the closest I've come to figuring out who did this to me." Her eyes turned steely. "If you guys are leaving, I'm coming, too."

Reena put a gentle hand on Jane's arm. "I know where you're coming from, we all do, but you don't even have your memory back. If what Takeda said is true, you could be traumatized by confronting your past before you're ready."

"Takeda?" It was the first time Ava had ever seen humor in Jane's eyes. "You're ready to leave right now. To dismiss everything he's done for you, everything he's taught you. But I'm supposed to stay and mind him like a good little girl." She shook her head. "I think I'll take my chances. Besides, if I don't remember who I am and what happened to me before you get your revenge, I'll never have a chance to get mine."

"She has a point," Jon said.

Cruz piped in. "And you never know. Maybe the real world is just what she needs. It might jog her memory or something."

Jane brushed the blond hair from her face. "Did I have a folder?"

Ava shook her head. "I'm sorry."

"It's okay," she said. "I should have expected it."

Jon rubbed his hands together. "Let's talk plans."

Cruz walked to the window, staring out into the darkness. "I think our first problem is pretty obvious."

"Getting off the island," Ava said.

Cruz nodded. "We need to get over a rather large body of water to return to the States. How do we plan to do that?"

Reena leaned her head on his shoulder, reminding Ava that they hadn't slept since the night before. There were very few clocks in the tera. They were encouraged to attend training sessions by following external cues—the position of the sun in the sky, the tide, the schedule of the tera staff. Still, Ava knew it had to be close to morning.

"I heard Takeda talking to one of his men about a plane," Jane said. "He mentioned a hangar on the other side of the cliff. From the conversation, I'm guessing it's a propeller plane."

Ava did a double take. "How do you know that?"

Jane shrugged. "The same way I know I can fly it."

CHAPTER SIXTEEN

"WHAT DO YOU MEAN YOU CAN FLY IT?" JON ASKED.
Jane's eyes clouded over as she tried to explain. "I . . .
just know. The same way I knew how big the plane was from
the way Takeda talked about the amount of fuel it needed."

"No offense," said Cruz, "but you don't remember your
own name. Now you know how to fly a plane?" He shook his
head. "Not sure that's a bet I'd take."

Reena glanced apologetically at Jane. "I kind of agree with
Cruz. It seems like a long shot."

"The roll, pitch, and yaw are the most important things.
The roll is the up-and-down motion of the wings, while the
pitch makes a plane descend or climb. That's what the eleva-
tors are for," Jane rattled off. Ava couldn't keep from staring
as Jane continued. "Lowering them causes the craft's nose to
drop, sending it into a descent. Raising them will compel the
airplane to climb. The yaw is the turning of the plane, which
is controlled by the rudder."

"I . . . what are you . . . ?" Reena started, unable to get the
rest of the words out.

"The rudder doesn't work alone," Jane continued. "It needs ailerons to make it turn. They raise and lower the wings."

The room fell silent, everyone staring at Jane in disbelief.

"You're quite the onion, aren't you?" Cruz finally said.

Jon nodded. "I'm good with her flying us out."

"Okay, then," Reena sighed, turning to Ava. "What about you, Winters? Are you in?"

She took in their faces, angry and driven, so reflective of her own betrayal. They were people of action. People who got things done. She, on the other hand, spent all her time thinking, weighing pros and cons from every angle until nothing got accomplished at all. Is that what she wanted? To sit around and train for revenge? To talk about it? To dream about it when she had an opportunity to actually *do* something about it?

She looked at the folders, holding their collective pasts. Her pain and loss had been reduced to nothing but words and pictures in Takeda's files. It was up to her to make sure they were remembered. Up to her to make sure the people who did it could never do it again.

Making up her mind, she spoke a single word.

No, not a word. A declaration.

"Fukushuu."

Cruz blanched. "What the hell is *fukushuu*?"

Jane nodded her understanding.

Ava looked at the others, meeting their eyes. "It means revenge."

"I'm sorry, Ms. Winters. I don't know what more to say," the bespectacled accountant says.

Tears stream down Ava's face as she sits in the Victorian-style office, the ornate décor contradicting the mundane tasks that occur within the accounting firm's off-white walls. She tries to explain that Charlie only had the power of attorney to sign their overseas land contract, not to sell Starling Vineyards.

But that's exactly what he did.

And, the accountant explains, the power of attorney allowed him to do it. Her naïveté allowed him to do it.

She tries to stop her hands from trembling but she's in a state of such absolute horror and disbelief that she feels outside of herself. Like she's watching it all happen to someone else.

"Are you all right, Ms. Winters?" the accountant asks. "Would you like me to call someone for you?"

The mention of her last name reminds her of something. "It was supposed to be Bay."

"I'm sorry?" The accountant's expansive forehead furrows.

"I was going to change my name to Bay this week," she explains.

"Well, at least we managed to prevent that fiasco."

Ava looks up at him. "What do you mean?"

He shifts uncomfortably in his padded chair. "Considering that he's not your husband, I mean."

Something cold slithers into Ava's heart. "What are you talking about?"

The man's face creases with regret. "I'm sorry. I thought you knew. A marriage license was never filed with the state in the names of Ava Winters and Charles Bay."

Ava stands on shaky legs, her head buzzing. Charlie was in charge of mailing the marriage papers. He told her it had *been done. And now she understood. He told her whatever she wanted to hear. Whatever would convince her that their love was real.*

"We had a wedding," she said weakly. "An officiant stood there and married us. His name was . . . Moore. Reverend Vance Moore."

"After our initial phone call, our office did some investigating. I'm sorry to say that Vance Moore was never ordained." His gaze softens. "But something tells me Mr. Bay already knew that."

Ava collapses in the chair, dropping her head in her hands. She doesn't cry. That would require emotion, feeling. And right now, there's nothing. Just numbness and a vast emptiness opening up inside her, bleak and dangerous.

The accountant comes around his desk, bending in front of her. "Is there anything I can do for you?"

She shakes her head, looking into his rheumy blue eyes. "I just don't understand. Charlie already had Starling Vineyards when he was with me. Why would he do this?"

He clears his throat. "I can only assume it was for profit, given that the estate was recently sold."

It's like a knife to the heart. Somehow it wasn't as bad thinking Charlie just wanted it. That maybe he wanted to walk the rows of grapes alone or sit on the terrace sampling the new Pinot.

But he didn't care about it at all.

She thinks of her grandmother, a wave of sorrow and regret nearly pulling her under. Sylvie would never have let this happen. Never did let it happen, despite all the offers thrown her way.

Ava sits up straighter, thoughts of her grandmother bringing her to something else.

"Tell me who purchased it," she demands, looking at the accountant.

He walks back to the desk and picks up a file, handing it to her. "A man by the name of William Reinhardt."

CHAPTER SEVENTEEN

THE HORIZON WAS TINGED PINK WHEN AVA EXITED her *washitsu*, scurrying along the perimeter of the shooting range. She moved confidently across the cold, hard ground. Now that she'd made the decision to join the others, there was no room for indecision. They had agreed to leave separately to avoid detection, meeting on the beach where they would make their way to the other side of the cliff.

All they could do was hope the plane was really there.

She had just rounded the corner of the training room when a voice broke through the faint light of dawn.

"Going somewhere?"

Ava turned toward the training room, seeing only shadows.

"Who's there?"

Emily Thorne stepped into the morning mist, draped in a white robe and holding an épée, one of the swords they used for fencing.

"I could use a dueling partner," Emily offered, twirling her épée in her hand. "I'd say I'd go easy on you, but that's never been my style."

"Thanks for the offer, but I'm actually heading out."

Emily nodded coolly. "Must be important. Don't let me keep you."

Ava shrugged. "See you around."

"That's going to be hard to do if you leave here," Emily said.

Ava stopped in her tracks.

"I have to say that I think it's a bad idea, Ava."

"You can't change my mind," Ava said stubbornly.

"I'm not trying to," Emily explained, "but it's a mistake to abandon this place before your training is done. Before you're ready."

Ava walked back to where Emily was standing; she didn't want to draw attention to herself by talking too loudly.

"We have a lead on the people who forced us down this path. And all of our missions are connected. We're going after our enemies as a team."

Emily hesitated. "I get that you're angry. I do. But being here will provide the guidance and discipline necessary to truly enact revenge."

Ava shook her head. She didn't want to hear it. She'd already agonized over the decision. Now that it was made, she didn't need Emily making her second-guess herself.

Emily met her eyes. "Ava. Trust me."

"I've trusted enough people," Ava hissed. "It's time to trust myself."

Emily seemed to consider Ava's words. "I think you know, deep down, that being here is what's best for you right now. It was for me."

"You don't get it," Ava said. "Do you know what it's like to trust someone and have him completely destroy your life?"

Emily nodded. "My father did. He trusted everyone. And because of that, both of our lives were ruined."

Ava shouldn't have been surprised by the confession. Why else would Emily be here if not for revenge? Isn't that why they were all here?

"I'm sorry," Ava said. "Your father . . . where is he now?"

Emily's eyes were unreadable as she shook her head. "It's been nearly twenty years, and thanks to Takeda, the people responsible for tearing down my father are finally beginning to get what they deserve. To do it right, to truly get your revenge, you have to do something even harder than figuring out how to trust again."

"What?" Ava asked.

"Have patience."

Ava thought about it, the logic of Emily's argument warring with the emotion that had mobilized her back in the meditation room. Everything Emily said made sense, but it didn't change anything. Ava had been the victim for too long. She wasn't waiting any longer.

"I appreciate your advice, Emily. Really, I do. But right now what we need—what I need—is action."

She turned and left, hurrying away from Emily before she could say anything else to try to change Ava's mind. Her past had been demolished, her legacy stolen.

The only thing left was revenge.

CHAPTER EIGHTEEN

AVA LOOKED OUT THE WINDOW, RUBBING THE broken piece of Acala's flame as the plane descended over Napa Valley's green knolls. The Hamptons might be the playground for the East Coast's rich, but Napa was the go-to refuge for California's most affluent. Celebrities, tech company billionaires, hotel socialites. They all came to Napa—both for the wine and a social calendar that put them front and center among the oldest West Coast money.

Ava cut a glance at Jane, seemingly at home in the cockpit of the propeller plane they'd appropriated from Takeda's hangar. The ride had been long, but surprisingly smooth. Jane had been right. She obviously knew what she was doing, even if she didn't know how she'd come into the knowledge.

Reena and Cruz looked out their windows, eyes fixated on the verdant landscape below, the grape fields overflowing with this year's crop.

Ava looked at Jon, finally awake after sleeping through most of the journey across the Pacific. He, too, turned his eyes downward, silent as the plane made its way closer to the ground. He glanced over at her, as he had felt her gaze. Their eyes locked, and for a moment, Ava wondered how long she would be able to deny her growing feelings for him.

She looked away. The answer was easy: as long as it took to exact revenge. She would never be able to give their mission her attention if she was distracted by a romantic relationship.

And there was no question which one was a priority.

Ava turned her eyes back to the window, the sky a brilliant cobalt tinged with yellow, a product of the endangered Contra Costa flowers that managed against all odds to flourish in wine country. She was hit with a rush of both longing and comfort. It wasn't the same. Would never be exactly the same. But this was home, and she was never going to let anyone take it from her again.

"I can't believe this is where you're from," Jon said, shaking his head.

"I definitely got lucky," Ava said, turning to him. "What about you? Where are you from?"

His laugh was harsh. "Stockton, originally."

She knew of it. Had seen the images on the news of the notoriously tough city. Geographically, it wasn't far from Napa's textured mountain ranges and flawless mansions, but it might as well have been a million miles away.

"So . . . why'd you move to Sonoma?" She knew she was pushing, but she couldn't seem to help herself. Despite all their late night conversations on the cliff, she still had the feeling that she didn't really know him.

"It was Courtney's idea," he said. "She wanted a better life for us."

"Did you find it?" The question escaped her lips before she could stop it. "I mean, before she . . . I'm sorry, I . . . probably should stop talking."

"Yeah, but where's the fun in that?" Cruz chimed in from the other side of the plane.

Ava shook her head, throwing Cruz a glare. Smart-ass.

She expected Jon to retreat back into his shell, but he surprised her by answering her question.

"We did. For a while."

"Ava?" Jane called her from the front of the plane. "Is that it?"

Ava looked out the window, seeking the old field that sat between the last acre of her former home and a historic, federal-style bed-and-breakfast. Abandoned for decades, the land was unsuitable for growing grapes and too far off the beaten path for anyone looking to build in a prestigious locale.

"That's it," Ava confirmed, spotting the empty field. "Next to that old house."

Jane made an adjustment and the plane angled downward.

"So what, exactly, is our plan?" Cruz asked. "Just barge into the big shindig on May first and confront these assholes?"

"That's exactly what we do," Reena said. "Force a confession."

But Ava knew it wouldn't be that easy. The Starling Gala was only two days away, but that didn't mean they were ready. They needed a plan. A real one.

She stared out the window, solemn and resolute. Even as the ground approached, it was hard to believe she was actually back in Napa. Just eight weeks earlier, she'd been departing for Japan, nervous and unsure what her training with Takeda would entail.

But as the plane touched the ground, bumping across the grassy field, she braced for something even scarier.

Coming home.

CHAPTER NINETEEN

"I JUST CAN'T BELIEVE YOU'RE REALLY HERE. IT'S SO good to see you, Ava."

Marie led them down the upstairs hallway. Her hair held more salt than pepper, the age lines around her eyes more deeply etched than they had been the last time Ava had seen her. But she still had the same warmth that made Marie's Inn a prime destination for the B&B set.

"I just appreciate your fitting us in on such short notice," Ava said, hit with a wave of nostalgia as she took in the familiar wallpaper, the artwork on the walls . . .

"Don't be silly," Marie said. "The season hasn't started yet. And I always have room for you."

She had been surprised to see them and even more surprised when she saw the plane sitting in her backyard. Still, she'd ushered them inside without hesitation, forcing them to catch their breath on the big sofas in the main living room while she brought them water and iced tea.

She stopped at the second door, bending to fit a key into the lock. The door swung open. "I'm afraid I only have three rooms available right now. I hope that will do."

"It will be fine," Reena said. "We appreciate your hospitality. Cruz and I can take this room, if that's all right."

Ava gaped. Where had this newly polite person come from and what had happened to the real Reena?

"Of course," Marie said, waving them in and handing Reena the key. "I serve coffee and pastries in the dining room starting at seven."

Cruz reached out to shake her hand. "Thank you."

They continued down the hall, leaving Jon in the next bedroom before coming to the last door.

"I guess this is us," Ava said to Jane as Marie opened the door.

Jane stepped into the room, her eyes traveling over the homey, vintage décor. "It's beautiful." She looked at Marie. "Thank you."

"It's my pleasure," Marie said. "Get some rest now. You look like you could use it." She hesitated. "Ava . . . I owe you an apology. It was wrong of me to assume—"

"No apology necessary. It was a totally understandable assumption," Ava said.

Marie shook her head. "Sylvie was like a mother to me. Your mom, one of my closest friends. I should have known you would never willingly sell Starling."

Ava took her hand. There was very little left of her old life, very few people who had stood by her. But Marie was one of them. She may have been upset when she'd heard about the sale of the vineyard, but she was here now when Ava needed her.

"It's okay," she said. "It's in the past. I'm here to move forward."

Marie leaned in, lowering her voice like she was afraid

someone would overhear even though the hallway was empty, the doors closed to the other rooms. "I see him sometimes, you know."

"Charlie?" Ava avoided Marie's eyes, some of the old shame creeping in. "Lucky you."

"William Reinhardt, too. Not that I get out much anymore. It's not like it used to be. All the parties and events seem to attract a different crowd these days." Marie looked around again. "I heard that he hires a different girl to be his date for every party."

"Reinhardt?" Ava was not surprised. "Probably because no one would be his date for free."

Marie nodded her agreement. "Everyone's real careful around him. They know what he's capable of."

"Because of what he did to me."

"Don't you worry about that," Marie said. "We know him for what he is now; nothing but a snake in the grass."

But taking that kind of bait would be a cop-out. Putting all the blame on Reinhardt or Charlie or anyone else wasn't going to get Ava anywhere. Part of revenge meant taking responsibility for her choices. Only then could she move past shame to action.

And that's exactly what she was going to do.

"He's a snake all right," Ava said. "But I'm the one who took a bite of the apple, and I'm the one who's going to make it right."

CHAPTER TWENTY

A VA LEANED AGAINST THE PORCH RAILING, breathing in the rich scent of soil. The sky was inky overhead, the half-moon casting golden light over the hills and fields surrounding the inn. It was nearly May, still early enough in the year to be mild, absent of the heat of mid to late summer that finishes the grapes just before harvest. A breeze rushed through the trees at the edge of the property, landing gently on Ava's skin, bare beneath the old-fashioned slip Marie had given her to sleep in.

She hadn't realized how much she missed it, had tried not to think about it. But it was home, and whatever Reinhardt had taken from her, whatever happened from here on out, that was something that would never change.

"Old habits die hard, huh?" Jon's voice came from behind her.

She turned, smiling a little. "I guess so. Can't sleep?"

He shook his head. "You?"

"I tried, but I guess I have too much on my mind."

He looked past the well-groomed front yard, planted with

flowers to attract paying guests, out over the fields in the distance.

"It must be weird, being back here."

She nodded. "It is. But also nice, despite everything."

"Home," he said simply.

"Yes."

They were silent for a moment, Ava painfully aware of his body next to hers, the fresh smell of soap suggesting a recent shower. He was wearing boxers and a T-shirt, snug enough to hint at his broad shoulders and muscled biceps. Her eyes were drawn to his hands, strong and sure on the porch railing. She had a flash of them on her bare waist, her hips.

She took a deep breath, shaking the image from her mind.

"What about you?" she asked, trying to get her mind on a different subject. "Does it feel weird to be back?"

He thought about it. "Well, this isn't home for me like it is for you, but it's close enough to dredge up the past. So I guess you could say it's weird."

She nodded her understanding. "On Rebun Island, all of this seemed so far away. I mean, I knew what I was training for, obviously. But it was all a little . . ."

He raised an eyebrow. "Abstract?"

She laughed softly, not wanting to wake the others. "Exactly. Now it's real."

His eyes locked with hers. "It's definitely real."

She wasn't sure if they were still talking about their plans, about revenge. He was only inches from her, so close she could feel the magnetic pull of his body. She suddenly had a hard time breathing, her breath coming fast and shallow, chest rising and falling as he reached a hand toward her face, tracing a

line from the rise of her cheekbone to the line of her jaw before twining his fingers in the hair at the back of her head.
She leaned into him, the crisp cotton of his T-shirt sending
sparks along the bare skin of her chest.

"Ava, I . . ."

And then his mouth was on hers, his lips warm and gentle
at first, building to an urgent demand as she kissed him back,
wrapping her arms around his back as he tipped her head to
plunder her mouth. She was lost, everything else forgotten
as she was pulled under by the desire roaring through
her body.

He moved his hand from the back of her head, letting
it travel down the side of her neck, over her bare shoulder.
Hooking a finger in the spaghetti strap of the slip, he started
to push it off her shoulder, his mouth finding the tender skin
of her collarbone.

Her head fell back as a moan escaped her lips. "Jon . . ."

And then, all at once, he was pulling back, returning her
strap to its full and upright position, putting cold space between their warm bodies.

She tried to shake off her passion-induced stupor. "What's
wrong?"

He shook his head. "I'm sorry. I'm . . . I can't . . ."

"Because of Courtney." It's not a question.

"It isn't right," he said, his eyes full of torment.

"She's gone, Jon," Ava said gently.

He nodded slowly. "That doesn't change the fact that I still
love her."

Ava's insides twisted. How could she fault him? He was a
good man, more loyal than any she'd ever known. Who was

JESSE LASKY

she to want more of him? To expect him not to mourn his dead fiancée?

"I understand." She reached out to touch his face, wanting to comfort him, then thought better of it. She let her hand drop. "Good night, Jon."

"Good night, Ava."

The words hit her back as she stepped into the house. She told herself that it was better this way, that they had more important things to worry about than their mutual attraction.

Then she told herself that she believed it.

CHAPTER TWENTY-ONE

"Y OU'RE STILL THE ONLY THING THAT SETTLES ME, Cruz," Reena said, lying naked next to him.

They had taken showers and settled into the room, falling into each other's arms with the combination of passion and familiarity that was uniquely theirs.

Cruz tenderly smoothed her hair. "At least we can do something now. Actually work to free Simon and bring justice to the bastards who murdered your mother and put him in prison."

Reena nodded, a sudden burst of fear flooding her body. "But what if something goes wrong?"

Cruz pulled away a little, tipping her face to his. "Are you telling me you're scared?"

"What? You're surprised?"

He pulled her naked body closer, kissing her head. "I'm not surprised you have doubts. Anyone would. I'm just surprised you'd let me know about them."

"I just . . . I don't want to fail," Reena said, running her hand along his bare chest. "And the truth is, I'm not even sure people will still care about my mother, about Simon. What if we get what we need to prove that Reinhardt, Cain, and Wells were responsible, but no one cares enough to pursue it?"

"We'll make them care," Cruz said. "We've come this far."

She looked up at him, touching his face. She'd perfected the art of holding people at bay, of making sure they didn't get close enough to really know her. But somehow Cruz had snuck in, found a way into the fortress of her heart. She'd be lost without him, something she didn't even dare think about for fear that it might come true.

Reena brought her face close to his. "You're a good man. The best." She kissed him gently, the uncertainty of the future bringing down the one remaining wall between them. "I love you, Cruz."

He looked at her with surprise, reaching up to touch her face. "You're full of surprises tonight, aren't you?" He continued without waiting for an answer. He kissed her deeply, passion rising between them again. "You already know I love you."

Reena smiled. "What makes you so sure?"

"Because," Cruz said, pulling her under him. "I followed you halfway around the world."

———————

CHAPTER TWENTY-TWO

The aroma of fresh rose petals and lavender winds its way into sixteen-year-old Jane's bedroom as she places the ruby earrings on her delicate lobes. She admires the earrings in the mirror, loving the way they shimmer in the glow from the Contra Costa goldfields outside her window.

Satisfied, she crosses the room and opens the closet door, stepping into a large walk-in lined with clothes. Designer jeans and tops hang on one side, rows of dresses and gowns on the other. Shoes, nestled in deep mahogany cubbies, stack the rear of the closet from floor to ceiling.

She scans the closet's offerings. Whatever she chooses will have to be just right.

As she sifts through the dresses—silk and taffeta and cotton and satin—something catches her eye on the wall. Pushing the dresses back, she leans in for a closer look, her gaze falling on a set of initials carved into the wall. She traces them with her fingertips, melancholy shrouding her heart even in the dream.

AVA WAS GONE WHEN JANE WOKE UP. SHE PADDED over to the window in her boxer shorts and tank top, perching on the window seat and trying to make sense of the strange dream. Or memory. Or whatever it was.

She couldn't have lived in Napa Valley. She'd have crossed paths with Ava, who seemed to know everyone and anything that happened in the contained world of the region's wineries and vineyards.

But then why did it seem so familiar? And it did seem familiar, although Jane couldn't put her finger on it when they'd first arrived. She had been exhausted from the flight, from the mental energy required to navigate the plane across the Pacific. All she had wanted was a hot bath and a soft bed.

But now, with the dream fresh in her mind, she was sure of it. She had been here before.

She considered her options. She could talk to Ava. Ask her if she remembered seeing Jane around Napa before she left. But that seemed stupid. If Ava had recognized her, she would have said something. At the very least, Jane would have seen the recollection in her eyes in some unguarded moment.

Wouldn't she?

But Jane was alone. More alone than any of the others. Reena and Cruz had each other, and it was obvious Ava and Jon had something going on, even if they tried to pretend it wasn't there.

Making a decision, Jane left the room. She walked down the hall, stopping in front of Cruz and Reena's room. Raising her hand to the door, she hesitated before finally knocking.

A few seconds later, Reena opened the door, dressed in jeans and a black T-shirt that hugged her lithe frame.

"Hey," she said. "Everything all right?"

"Can I . . . Can I talk to you?" Jane asked.

Reena nodded, concern crossing her blue eyes. "Cruz is still sleeping. Let's go downstairs."

She closed the door behind her. They followed the scent of coffee and baked goods to a sideboard in the dining room loaded with coffee, tea, and an assortment of pastries, muffins, and scones. Reena made herself a cappuccino and chose a vanilla scone while Jane poured water for tea.

"You should eat," Reena said, casting an eye at Jane's tea.

She shook her head. "I'm not hungry."

"I know, but it's important to take care of yourself, especially now."

Jane smiled. "I'll get something later, I promise."

They made their way to the living room and settled on two wing chairs facing a chintz-covered sofa. Reena sipped at her cappuccino, waiting patiently for Jane to start. Cradling her cup, letting the warmth of her tea seep into her hands, Jane thought about how to begin.

"I think I've been here before," she finally said.

"Marie's Inn?"

Jane shook her head. "Napa Valley or . . . Northern California, maybe? It just . . . it's so familiar."

"Maybe it's just being back in the States," Reena suggested.

"It's not like that. The air, the way it smells . . . The way everything . . . feels." She took a deep breath. "I've lived here before. I'm sure of it."

CHAPTER TWENTY-THREE

STEPPING OUT OF THE SHOWER, AVA TOWELED OFF and slipped into a pair of gray khakis tied at the ankle and a white T-shirt, two of the few things she'd brought with her when she left Rebun Island. She picked up the piece of Acala's flame from the dresser and put it in her pocket.

She'd grown used to carrying it around.

She'd expected to toss and turn, her kiss with Jon front and center in her mind. Instead, she'd fallen into the deepest sleep she'd had since leaving the Valley. Apparently, even her subconscious knew she was home.

She went back to her room and combed out her hair, leaving it to dry in waves around her face. Then she slipped her feet into a pair of white sneakers. She sat there for a minute, drinking in the warmth of the sun slanting across the down comforter on the four-poster bed. She thought about Jon, about what had happened—and almost happened—between them on the porch. She couldn't leave it that way. Whatever else there was or wasn't between them, he was her friend.

And they had work to do.

She went out into the hallway and made her way to his

room, knocking softly on the door. She crossed her arms nervously over her chest while she waited. A few seconds passed, then a minute.

Nothing.

She knocked again, louder this time, wondering if he'd gone down to get breakfast. But that didn't make sense. It was only seven thirty. They had been up late, and Jon was known for being the anti-morning person. It was one thing to be up early when Takeda was waiting for them in the training room, another to be up early without reason.

She reached for the doorknob, testing it, surprised to find it unlocked. Biting her lip, wondering if she was doing the right thing, she turned it. The door swung open, the room seemingly empty.

Ava stepped inside, wondering if Jon was in the bathroom. "Jon?" she called out softly, heading for the half-open door of the private restroom. "I wanted to talk to you about last night."

But she knew he wasn't there. There was something vacant and vacuous behind the door, the feeling of a room devoid of human presence. She pushed open the door, unsurprised to find it empty.

She was turning to leave the room when she caught sight of a piece of paper on the floor near the writing desk. Crossing the room, she bent to pick it up, realizing it was a background sheet on Frederick Cain, exactly like the one in her file.

Straightening, she looked on the writing desk, wanting to return the paper to the folder.

It was gone.

She looked around the room, wondering if Jon had moved the folder to one of the nightstands or to the dresser. But the room was as clean and empty as it had been when they'd arrived. Even Jon's bag and clothes were gone.

Ava hurried out of the room and down the stairs, stopping at the front desk, where Cruz was standing with Marie.

"Have you seen Jon?"

Cruz started to shake his head but was interrupted by Marie. "Jon . . . the tall one?"

Ava nodded.

"He left a couple of hours ago, bright and early. Hadn't even made the coffee."

"Did he say where he was going?" she asked.

"Not really, but he did ask me how far it is from here to St. Luke's Hospital."

"Ava?" Cruz asked. "What's going on?"

Ava ignored the question. "St. Luke's? That's in Windsor. In Sonoma County."

"That's right," Marie said.

Ava turned her attention to Cruz. "Where are Reena and Jane?"

Now there was concern in his eyes. "In the living room."

She turned to Marie. "Can we borrow your car?"

CHAPTER TWENTY-FOUR

THE MAYACAMAS MOUNTAINS LOOMED OVER THEM as they made their way toward Sonoma, Cobb Mountain, the tallest in the range, stalking them from behind.

Ava was in the driver's seat of Marie's four-door with Reena riding shotgun, Cruz and Jane in the back. As they left Napa behind, the landscape slowly began to change. Upscale boutiques and bistros gave way to blue-collar bars and corner liquor stores. It was uncharted territory, and Ava realized with a twinge of guilt that in all the time she had lived in Napa, she'd never once been to this part of the region.

"So explain to me again why this is a big deal?" Cruz asked.

"He took his folder, Cruz, and all of his belongings. I don't know what he's doing, but it has to do with what happened to Courtney. And it doesn't seem like he plans on coming back."

"Is that any of our business?"

Reena made a disgusted sound. "He's one of us, Cruz. We can't just let him go off half-cocked, getting himself killed. Besides, our missions are entwined. We're in this together, remember?"

"I guess," he said. "It just seems to me that if a man wants to take matters into his own hands, it's his prerogative."

Nobody said anything, and forty minutes later they pulled into the parking lot at St. Luke's. As they hurried toward the front of the hospital, Ava's mind started working the possible obstacles to finding Jon, another of Takeda's many lessons.

"How are we going to find out where he is?" she asked as they stepped through the automatic doors. "He could be any-where."

"Allow me," Cruz said, strolling up to a nurse behind the main counter.

"What's he going to do?" Jane asked Reena.

She shrugged, an admiring smile playing on her lips. "The guy was an aspiring politician. This is what he does. He'll talk, she'll eat it up."

"Do you ever worry about what Takeda said?" Jane asked.

"What are you talking about exactly?"

But Ava knew exactly where Jane was headed. She'd thought about it herself with Jon.

"Your feelings for Cruz," Jane continued. "Takeda said emotions get in the way. Make you weak. Make you vulnerable."

Ava caught a flash of fear in Reena's eyes in the moment before her expression turned impassive. "Takeda may know a lot of things, but he doesn't know Cruz. He's indestructible."

"Okay guys," Cruz said, returning from the front desk. "Jon's registered as a visitor. ICU Room 402."

Ava was baffled. "ICU?"

Cruz nodded. "Come on. It's upstairs."

They headed for the elevator and made their way to the fourth floor. They were on their way past the nurse's station when they were stopped by a Nurse Ratched look-alike. At first, Ava worried they wouldn't be able to get past her, but then Cruz pulled her aside, speaking to her in low tones, and a minute later, they were allowed past.

"What did you say to her?" Jane asked.

Cruz just smirked.

Room 402 was at the end of the hall. They stopped at the wall of glass fronting the room and peered inside. A large window flooded the room with light, providing a view of the slow-moving waters of Putah Creek just beyond Route 175.

Ava scanned the room, stopping at a still figure standing next to the bed.

Jon.

An EKG machine stood next to the bed, green peaks and valleys displayed across its screen. Ava's gaze slid to the person in the bed, a shrunken woman with a large bandage around her forehead and skin so pale it was almost translucent. It took Ava only a minute to understand.

She stepped into the room, making her way quietly to where Jon stood.

"Courtney," Ava said softly. "She never died."

"Her parents refuse to face reality," Jon said, reaching toward the lifeless body of the woman in the bed. He stroked her light brown hair. "But I know she's gone."

His voice was tender, his eyes glazed as he looked at her. Before Ava could check the emotion, she was awash in sorrow, not only for Jon's sadness, and Courtney's obviously devastating injury, but for the lost possibility between her and Jon. He would be a prisoner to his grief forever.

She was immediately racked by guilt. She wouldn't wish

this kind of loss on anyone, not even her enemies on whom she sought vengeance. And she and Jon needed to focus on their mission anyway. Courtney was a necessary reminder of that.

"I'm sorry, Jon," Ava said softly.

Reena, Cruz, and Jane eased into the doorway behind her.

"I'm sorry, man," Cruz said, touching Jon's back. "Will she ever wake up?"

"The bullets, when they pierced her skull . . ." Jon sighed in anguish. "I don't know. But what I do know is that I'm going to make the people responsible get what they deserve."

He bent to kiss Courtney's face, then grabbed his jacket and headed for the door.

"Wait!" Ava put her hand on his arm. "Where are you going?"

Jon just looked at her. "You don't get it, Ava. I did this to her."

Ava shook her head. "What are you talking about?"

Jon stared into her eyes. "I was working for Cain. That's why he went after Courtney. So if you're looking for revenge against Cain and his men, maybe you should think about coming after me, too."

He walked out of the room, leaving the rest of them standing in stunned silence.

CHAPTER TWENTY-FIVE

JANE HEARD AVA AND JON TALKING, SAW REENA and Cruz watching. But everything faded into the background as she focused on Courtney, lying in the hospital bed.

Something was picking at the back of her mind. A nagging certainty that she could almost grasp. A kind of déjà vu that was part recollection, part daydream.

Then, all at once, she wasn't in the hospital room anymore. She was somewhere else completely, lost to the present, prisoner to her forgotten past.

Jane is seventeen, lying in a hospital bed surrounded by stark white walls. Her eyes flicker—back and forth, open and shut.

She's scared.

Jane can sense that she's hooked up to the beeping machines at her side, a net of electrodes smothering the parts of her face that haven't been badly bruised, critically battered. The stitches on Jane's cheek continually itch and burn, but she doesn't make a sound as she floats in and out of consciousness.

Someone approaches her bed, coming to a stop next to

*her. She feels a pair of eyes on her face, but when she tries
to see who it is, she only gets a blurry vision that could be a
man or a woman. Whoever it is sobs softly, apologizing over
and over.*

*Apologizing for having done this to her, for having put
her here.*

*Jane tries her best to stay awake, but one question pounds
at her brain, more painful than the fractures and lacerations
covering her body.*

How is she still alive?

*The mystery person leans over, pressing gentle lips to her
forehead. Jane's eyes flicker open, the figure, turning and
leaving the room, still blurry.*

Jane came to consciousness with a jolt of cold, ice raining
down on her as Cruz held a plastic container in his hands.

Reena's face loomed over her. "Jane? It's all right, Jane.
You're okay. You're okay."

Jane's breath came fast and heavy, the memory still fresh
in her mind. She clutched at Reena's arms, trying to hold on
to the details. Was the person weeping responsible for her
condition? Was that person behind the wheel of the car she
saw in her dream?

"What happened?" she finally asked.

Reena shook her head. "I don't know. One minute you
were standing there, fine, and the next you were screaming
and shouting, falling to the floor."

Cruz studied her face. "Did you remember something?"

Jane thought about the vision. Was it all coming back to

her? Had Courtney's hospital room triggered a memory of her own?

"I . . . I don't know. I'm so sorry. " She got to her feet, looking around the room. "Wait a minute . . . Where's Jon? Where's Ava?"

CHAPTER TWENTY-SIX

FREDERICK CAIN LIFTED THE GLASS OF TWENTY-one-year-old Lagavulin, polishing it off in a single gulp. He found it ironic that in Latin, whisky translated to "water of life."

Especially given his occupation as a killer for hire.

Not that he lost any sleep over the trail of death in his wake. Everybody had to make a living somehow.

He took a deep breath, leaning over the old mahogany bar inside Tavern Red. It was a hole in the wall, closed to the public until five o'clock and under the radar of everyone but hard-core locals and the very few people who knew where to find Cain. It worked well as a front for his operation. In fact, business was booming.

A few of his men finished pints of beer in a booth at the back while two others, Vic and Lee, played pool in the corner. Vic leaned down, aiming for the corner pocket. The ball missed by a hair.

"I think I'm going to be twenty dollars richer by the end of this game," Lee said, stroking his beard as he surveyed the table, lining up his next shot.

Another day, another dollar.

Cain tapped the bar. The young bartender, slicing limes with a wicked blade, put down his knife and gave Cain another generous pour of Lagavulin. He was returning the bottle to its place behind the bar when the sound of a phone ringing cut through the silence.

Everyone paused, all eyes on Cain. At Tavern Red, a ringing phone in the middle of the afternoon could only mean two things: a job gone wrong or a job coming in.

Cain swallowed the liquor in his glass and removed his phone from the pocket of his perfectly tailored Italian suit.

"Hello?"

"I expect to see you on Saturday. You do know that, don't you?"

Cain wasn't surprised to hear William Reinhardt's voice on the other end of the line.

"I told you," Cain said coldly, "it's not my scene."

"Irrelevant," Reinhardt retorted. "You're not invited to dazzle me with your witty repartee."

Cain was unmoved. "Tell your buddy the senator that if he wants to talk to me, he has my number. And for him, I'll consider picking up."

"You know Wells doesn't like to discuss business over the phone. Or through email."

"So the guy's paranoid. The way he got into office, I don't blame him."

Reinhardt's voice was muffled as he said something to someone on the other end of the phone. When he came back, he lowered his voice. "Wells wants to meet in person. He has located him."

Cain laughed with satisfaction.

"The party is the perfect cover," Reinhardt says smoothly. "You'll be just two guests of many, and if you come at ten, everyone will be too drunk off vintage port to remember who was conversing with whom."

Cain thought about it. He and Reinhardt had known each other a long time, their relationship mutually beneficial far beyond their imaginations. Their history could either catapult them to further success—or consign them to prison. Cain might not be sitting in a tony vineyard in Napa, but he was smart enough to know that it was better to pacify than to alienate a person like Reinhardt.

"Tomorrow at ten, huh?" he asked.

"I'll see you then."

CHAPTER TWENTY-SEVEN

Ava sits, devouring a warm meal at St. Ella's Women's Shelter of Carson City, Nevada, about two hundred miles northeast of Napa Valley. The shelter's low-hanging ceiling and dreary walls reflect the feelings of the women huddled in the tight space. Trapped and full of despair, this is the end of the line.

Ava, her beauty hidden behind tired eyes, is in a constant state of confused anxiety. She's been on the streets for almost a year, having sold most of her mother's and grandmother's jewelry and clothes to survive, a piece of her heart breaking off each and every time.

But she was only able to get her hands on so much, and it's all gone now anyway.

Ava tries to make the corn bread and thin soup served by the shelter last. She doesn't want them to ask her to leave. As she takes a scoop of food, she notices a loose thread from her ripped, fingerless glove and attempts to tear it off, but instead of a clean break, the donation bin glove begins to unravel. The sight of it causes an irrational tear to spill onto Ava's cheek. She takes a deep breath, trying to get it together.

She just can't seem to catch a break.

Just then, a man sits down at her table. He's rugged, good-looking, and the only person in the run-down building who seems in control. It's obvious he doesn't belong there, but then again, neither does Ava, something he lets her know when he speaks a moment later.

"This isn't the life you're supposed to have." He leans in close to her. "And I know how to help you get it all back."

A VA DROVE LIKE A BAT OUT OF HELL, HOPING SHE was right. Once she'd recovered from the shock of Jon's confession, she'd hurried to the car, flipping frantically through her file, looking for anything that might tell her where Jon might go in search of Cain. She'd found it in a report on Cain's business holdings: a down-and-out bar called Tavern Red on the wrong side of town, reportedly Cain's informal headquarters.

She could only assume that's where Jon was headed. If he wasn't there, she would have to resign herself to the fact that he might be lost to her and the others.

She pulled up outside the bar, spotting Jon right away. He was standing outside, surveying the mission-style building under a sun that was baking the already-hard ground. Ava had seen a gas station a mile back, and more recently, an abandoned warehouse. Other than that, they were in the middle of nowhere, nothing but stray cats roaming and trash tumbling across the dusty ground.

He was heading inside, his stride purposeful, when she leapt from the car, running toward him with all the speed she could muster.

"Jon!" she called out. "Stop!"

He kept walking, seemingly oblivious to her voice.

She grabbed on to his arm, trying to pull him to a stop. But it was like trying to hold on to a Mack truck in high gear. All of Takeda's training couldn't make up for the fact that Jon outweighed her by a good hundred pounds, an advantage that was only magnified by his determination.

He tried to shake her off. "Let go of me, Ava."

"Please," she begged. "You can't stop these people this way."

"It's none of your business," he said, his brown eyes cold. "I need to do this. It's the only way to make things right."

She took hold of his arm again. "If this is about last night . . . if you feel guilty . . ."

"Last night has nothing to do with this!" he shouted.

She reached up, putting her hands on his face, forcing him to look at her, ignoring the connection that crackled between them even now.

"You feel guilty," she said. "For living, for feeling, while Courtney can't. I get that. But being stupid isn't going to solve anything. If you want to make them suffer the way you have—the way Courtney has—this isn't the way."

"That's all you do, Ava. All any of you do; talk and think. And talking and thinking isn't going to give Courtney the justice she deserves."

"We're supposed to be a team!" she yelled. "If you do this, you're making the decision for all of us."

Jon pushed past her, heading for the door of Tavern Red.

She stepped in front of him, putting a hand on his chest. "Please."

"Step aside, Ava." His voice was flat and cold, no sign of the affection and friendship that had grown between them.

"They'll kill you."

His eyes burned through her with dire conviction. "Then so be it."

Ava was trying to think of something to say, anything that might get Jon to listen to reason, when an ominous thud sounded behind them.

Ava turned and found herself staring into the barrels of two cocked pistols. One of them was held by a massive guy with arms like tree trunks. The other by a man with a beard, his head shaved clean.

"Well, well, well," the guy with the beard said. "Look what the cat dragged in."

CHAPTER TWENTY-EIGHT

"$\mathcal{S}$O," THE BIGGER GUY SAID, "TO WHAT DO WE OWE this pleasure?"

They had forced Ava and Jon inside, tying them to two chairs in the middle of the pub. The two men still pointed guns their way, but other than that, the mood was calm. Too calm. An older man sat with his back to them at the bar, and a group of men sat calmly at a back table as if Ava and Jon weren't being held at gunpoint in the middle of the room.

The man with the beard—Ava thought she had heard the other guy call him Lee—smacked Jon in the face with the butt of his gun.

"Are you deaf? I asked you what you were doing here. How did you find us?"

Jon didn't say anything, his face impassive as blood trickled from a cut on his temple. He closed his eyes as the man named Lee raised his gun to hit him again.

"Lee, Vic," the man at the bar called to them. "Come here."

Vic waved the gun at Jon and Ava. "Don't even think about moving."

"Don't say anything to them, Ava," Jon whispered as they walked away. "No matter what they do to me."

Halfway to the bar, the big man named Vic turned back, leering at Ava, but talking to Jon. "She's not bad, West. Although I have to say, I'm kind of surprised you brought us another girl after what happened to the last one."

Jon thrashed in the chair, an expression of pure fury on his face.

Vic neared Jon again, pressing the gun against Jon's still-bleeding temple. "Courtney, right? Was that her name? How's she doing, anyway?" Vic's finger rested on the trigger. "I guess you'll find out soon enough."

"Cain!" Jon yelled. "Why don't you stop hiding behind your hired goons and come do your own dirty work?"

Ava's head snapped up, her attention drawn to the man at the bar. So that was Frederick Cain. The hired killer who had murdered Reena's mother for Jacob Wells.

Vic kept his eyes on Jon as he called out to Cain, still at the bar. "Hey, boss, can I waste this guy?"

Cain didn't even turn around. He just raised a hand, his back still to them. "As long as you clean up your mess."

Vic aimed the gun, level with Jon's head, as Ava looked around, frantically searching for a way to help Jon, to get them both out of this mess.

She was bracing herself for the explosion of gunfire when something came swinging from the rafters, crashing on top of Vic.

Not something. Someone.

It was Jane, her momentum knocking Vic to the floor, where he lay unconscious. Ava stared at her in shock. Jane was hardly recognizable, her hair wild, her face expressionless and cold.

She turned toward Jon and Ava, whipping a knife out of her belt and cutting the ropes that bound them as Cain and Lee rose from the bar.

Lee pointed his firearm at Jane, but before he could squeeze off a shot, the large open window to his right shattered, glass falling to the ground like rain as Reena catapulted through it, crashing into him.

The gun flew out of his hand, landing just inches from Ava's feet, and all at once her mind started working again, Takeda's training taking over as she bent to pick up the weapon. The metallic barrel was cool to the touch, the rubber grip firm as she wrapped her hand around it.

Ava was surprised to see Cruz. She hadn't seen him enter the bar in the commotion. He headed straight for the bar and Reena, landing a wicked punch to Lee's face, knocking him out as Cain turned toward Jon and Ava.

Cruz registered the chaos around him. "We really should've slept in," he said dryly, jumping onto the bar and launching himself at Cain.

Cruz slammed him against the bar. "You don't recognize me, do you?"

Cain was surprisingly calm. "Should I?"

Reena moved next to Cruz, grabbing Cain's arm and twisting it behind his back. "What about me?" she asked. "Recognize me?"

Recognition lit his eyes. "You're that senator's daughter."

"Yeah," she said. "The senator you had killed."

The man named Vic groaned, writhing on the ground as

he gained consciousness. Jon moved in, slamming his foot into the man's back, sending him sprawling back to the terra-cotta tiled floor.

"Don't even think about it," Jon said. He looked at Ava. "I've got this guy. See if the others need help."

Ava looked around, spotting two men approaching from behind Cruz and Reena, who were still holding Cain against the bar. Remembering the men who had been drinking at the table in the back, Ava shouted a warning.

"Cruz! Behind you!"

But she shouldn't have worried. Jane was on it, using the kicking and punching techniques Takeda had taught them to keep the men at bay. Cruz moved in to help but was quickly sidelined by three broad-shouldered men armed with pool cues.

Remembering the gun she was holding, Ava turned it on them, power moving like liquid ice through her veins. The gun felt good in her hands. Solid. Finally, she was in control.

The men froze, staring at the gun aimed their way.

"How does it feel?" she asked them. "I could kill you right now, just like you've killed for that bastard you call your boss."

She contemplated doing it. Pulling the trigger and delivering justice in one shot.

"Ava . . ." Cruz's voice was a warning. "Don't do it. This isn't how we were trained."

Over by the bar, Jane grabbed one of the men and slammed his head into the jukebox as Reena held a knife to Cain's throat, her face distorted by rage as she tried to get him talking.

"Admit what you did!" she screamed. "Admit it or I'll kill you!"

But Cain must have had nerves of steel, because he remained silent, his face pressed up against the bar, a rivulet of blood running down his neck as the knife in Reena's hand nicked his skin.

And then, someone else appeared, rising like a shadow from behind the bar. The bartender, Ava realized. He moved quickly, grabbing the knife out of Reena's hand in one swift movement.

But it was more than the activity that had Ava's attention. She was frozen, her eyes glued to the bartender's face.

What the hell was *he* doing here?

The momentary distraction was all Cain's men needed. One of them lunged for her, knocking the gun from her hand as they both hit the floor. The gun slid across the tile, out of reach, as Ava kicked the monster off her with a move she'd learned during her third week on Rebun Island.

Jon and Cruz moved in, punching the other two men while Jane jumped on one of the tables, scanning the room like she was trying to get her head around all that was happening.

And then, everything seemed to slow down as Cain's eyes stopped on Jane's face, his expression turning to one of disbelief.

"My God. It can't be . . . ," he said.

Wait a minute . . . Did Cain recognize Jane?

Jane, oblivious to the recognition in Cain's eyes, flipped off the table, dealing quick, lethal blows to the last two of Cain's men still standing.

Takeda's group of revenge-seekers stood, breathing heavy and surveying the carnage, until the sound of rusted metal scraping against concrete screamed through the air.

Ava turned with the others toward the back door, where Cain, taking advantage of the chaos, was making his escape.

Jon took off like a shot.

"Jon! Don't!" Ava called out.

Reena shoved the bartender off her and sprinted after Jon. Ava wasn't surprised to see the bartender step aside now that the danger had passed. Jane's gaze locked on him, and for a moment, Ava wondered if Jane recognized him, too.

Ava's attention was pulled away from them as Lee stumbled up from the floor, blood pouring from his skull. She only had time to shout as he reached for the gun lying on the floor near one of the tipped-over tables.

"The gun!"

But it took him only a second to raise the weapon, pointing it at Reena as she chased after Cain with Jon. Lee squeezed the trigger.

"Reena, no!" Cruz screamed, lunging for her, pivoting his body in front of her just as he did on the cliff on Rebun Island.

The bullet slammed into his chest. He froze, shock written all over his face as he looked at the wound on his chest, already seeping red. A second later, another shot roared through the air, piercing his skin two inches to the right of the first shot.

Cruz was down.

CHAPTER TWENTY-NINE

REENA'S SCREAM TORE THROUGH THE AIR AS CRUZ fell to the floor. She dropped next to him, cradling his head in her lap.

"No, no, no . . . ," she muttered, touching his face. "You can't do this to me, Cruz. I need you." Her voice rose. "Do you hear me? I need you! You can't go!"

Two more gunshots ripped through the shocked silence. Ava was so disoriented by everything that had happened—by everything that was still happening—that it took her a minute to trace the shots to the bartender's gun. She followed his gaze and saw Lee, crumpled on the floor, the gun that had felled Cruz still in his hand.

A crash sounded near the bar as Vic tried to stand, knocking glasses to the floor as he staggered to his feet. A second later, he lurched for the back door, following his boss out into the hot Sonoma afternoon.

"Come on, Cruz," Reena said. "It's time to wake up now. We still have work to do. Simon needs you. *I* need you."

His face was gray, his eyes closed. Ava lifted his wrist, feeling for a pulse. When she couldn't find one, she lowered her head to his chest, listening in vain for his heartbeat.

Ava took a deep breath and laid a hand on Reena's shoulder. "He's gone."

No one moved, Reena's quiet sobbing the only sound in the once-chaotic tavern. Ava was surprised to feel the ache of something unfamiliar, almost forgotten: loss. She didn't think she could feel it anymore. Didn't think she was capable of caring about anyone enough for it to matter if something happened to him.

But somehow, they had become comrades in arms. The loss of Cruz and Reena's heartache sat like a stone on Ava's chest.

Suddenly, two more gunshots sounded, muffled this time, coming from outside.

"Jon!" Ava jumped to her feet, crossing the room and grabbing the weapon in Lee's lifeless hand.

She looked from Jane to Reena, hesitant to leave her after all that had happened. But Reena just nodded.

"I'm fine. Go."

Ava knew it was a lie. It would be a long, long time before Reena was fine. But losing Jon wouldn't change what had happened to Cruz.

"I'll stay," Jane said, dropping to the floor next to Reena. "Go get those bastards."

She was almost to the back door when a familiar voice called to her from the bar.

"Don't do this, Ava," the bartender said.

"Don't try to stop me, Shay." She raced toward the exit, the weapon surprisingly comfortable in her hand.

Bursting into the alleyway behind Tavern Red, she looked around, trying to find the source of the gunshots. The sun was low in the sky, shrouding the alley in shadow, a lone Dumpster the only possible hiding spot for Cain.

She made her way toward it, gun drawn. Creeping up on the hulking piece of orange metal, she placed her back against it, preparing herself to come face-to-face with the barrel of a gun. But when she looked behind the Dumpster, weapon extended in front of her, no one was there.

Tires screeched from the end of the alley, pulling Ava's attention away from the Dumpster. She ran toward the noise, spotting a black Lincoln racing away from Tavern Red. She could make out Jon's head in the passenger seat, which meant Cain must be driving.

She ran after the car, but only managed a few steps before nearly tripping over something. Stumbling, she looked down to see a body lying facedown in the dirt, surrounded by blood.

The Lincoln long gone, Ava bent down and turned the body over, coating her hands in blood.

It was Frederick Cain.

But then who took Jon?

She didn't have long to consider the question as a viselike hand wrapped around her neck from behind.

"Now it's your turn, bitch." Ava dimly recognized Vic's voice as he pressed her against the harsh metal of the Dumpster, forcing the life out of her.

She was only scared for a minute. Then her fear turned to anger. Anger that she wouldn't get to finish her path of revenge.

That she wouldn't be able to make Reinhardt and Charlie pay for what they did to her.

What they did to all of them.

But even her anger was short-lived, followed by a sweet flood of tranquility as she began to lose consciousness.

Now she didn't have to fight. She could just let go.

CHAPTER THIRTY

J ANE GRABBED THE BARTENDER'S ARM AS HE HUR-
ried after Ava.

"Who are you?" she demanded, studying his face, trying to figure out why the dark hair and ice-blue eyes seemed so familiar.

He hesitated. "Let go, Jane."

She kept hold of his arm. "How do you know to call me that?"

He moved so fast, flipping her over on to her back, that she didn't even see it coming.

And there was something else; Jane knew that move. They all did.

He pressed one black boot against Jane's neck as she lay beneath him. It was heavy, rigid, and put her in an inescapable state of immobilization. But she sensed restraint in his muscular legs. He was being careful, trying not to hurt her.

"Stay still. And stay here." He looked from Jane to Reena, his voice low and rough. "I need to go after Ava, but it's not safe. Do you understand? You need to stay in here until I get back."

And then he was gone, leaving them both to wonder how he knew them. And how he knew Takeda.

CHAPTER THIRTY-ONE

"You said you know my story. How?" Ava asks the stranger at the shelter.

He tells her it's not important how he's come to know her story. What's important is doing something about it. He wants to know what Ava's been doing to get Starling Vineyards back. What she plans to do to right the wrongs committed against her.

She blanches, shrinking in her seat. As far as she's concerned, there's nothing she can do about it.

"Is there something you'd like to do?"

Ava's heart thuds excitedly at the possibility. It's not about the estate or the money. It's about what it symbolizes. About the fact that people she trusted betrayed her as if she meant nothing, treated her life like some kind of game that they've now won.

Talking to Shay, she moves past heartbreak to red-hot anger.

"So what do you really want?" he asks her.

"I want to make them pay."

"You're talking about fukushuu," he tells her.

Ava doesn't even know what that means. She doesn't care. She just wants to know who sent him.

Shay leans forward. "His name is Takeda. Satoshi Takeda."

Shay says he can help her, his voice growing low to avoid the surrounding women, all of whom are in need of a hot meal on a cold night. He explains that Takeda specializes in the sort of retribution Ava wants, even if she hasn't fully realized she wanted it until now.

"Not a second goes by where I don't consider going after the people who did this to me," she confides.

"Then why don't you?"

Ava considers his question. She explains that she has no means. No expertise.

But Shay does. More importantly, Takeda does.

"I don't know about this . . . ," Ava says.

"Sure you do. Otherwise you wouldn't still be sitting here with me."

"So you're going to take me to Japan?"

"No, I need to stay here."

"How can I trust you?"

"Because I know what you've been through," Shay tells her. "And the fact that no one's investigated the bastards who conned you out of your life, who show no remorse or regard for you or your family . . . Well, that's why I'm doing this instead of still . . ."

"Instead of what?" she asks him, intrigued.

He shook his head. "It's not important. What's important is that I want to help. Takeda wants to help." He pauses. "Close your eyes."

"What? Why?"

"Just do it," he says gently. "Trust me."

After a brief hesitation, she closes her eyes, although it will be a long time before she really trusts anyone again.

"Now think of those who wronged you," he says. "Think of what they did to you. What they took from you."

Ava's lungs become heavy, her pulse racing as adrenaline hits her system. She's tired of running. Tired of being afraid. Of moving from town to town, wondering how long it will be before the little she's managed to scrape together will be taken from her again. She sees now that she's scarred, damaged, afraid to live.

And because of that, she's not living at all.

She welcomes the anger building in her heart, lets it push out the vulnerability and fear that has resided there since Charlie and Reinhardt stole her legacy.

Finally, she opens her eyes.

"Tell me, Ava Winters," he says, "what do you really want?"

She doesn't hesitate. "Revenge."

He smiles. "Then you've got a plane to catch."

AVA WAS ALMOST COMPLETELY UNDER, SWIMMING toward the dark ocean of unconsciousness, when she saw Shay out of the corner of one barely open eye.

The next thing she knew, he grabbed hold of Vic's collar, hauling him off Ava like he was nothing but a child.

"No," she protested, trying to find her way back to the peaceful calm. "Leave me alone. Let me go . . ."

"Bullshit," Shay said, tossing Vic to the ground and pulling Ava to her feet. "Get up."

Blackness raced in from all sides as she rose, dizziness threatening to send her back to the ground. She leaned against the Dumpster, calling out a warning as Vic stood behind Shay.

"Behind you!"

Shay turned, ducking under Vic's jab and rising to deliver a swift blow to the man's stomach. The hit brought Vic to his knees. Ava watched as Shay nailed him with an elbow to the head, causing him to collapse against the Dumpster. He fell to the ground, out cold.

Shay turned to face her. She glared at him, gingerly touching her neck, which was tender and already swollen.

"You're not supposed to be here," she choked from her burning throat.

"You're welcome," Shay said through gritted teeth.

"I'm supposed to thank you now?"

"For saving your ass?" he nodded. "Yeah. 'Thank you' seems appropriate."

"I didn't ask for your help," she said.

"Yeah, well, I'll chalk that up to an oversight on your part. Like everything else you guys did today."

Anger flooded her body, replacing the apathy that had made her complacent just moments before. "What are you talking about?"

"This wasn't part of the plan," he said.

"None of this was *your* plan," she said. "It was *our* plan."

"Dying in an alleyway?" he fumed. "That was your plan?"

She was quiet, his words hitting a nerve as she remembered the strange comfort she'd felt as she slid toward death. The sweet release of knowing she didn't have to fight anymore.

Didn't have to plot or plan. Didn't have to be afraid that she would never, ever find herself again.

"What happened to you?" he said softly. "You used to be a fighter."

She turned away, ashamed at the tears stinging her eyes. "I'm tired."

She was standing there, her back to Shay as she tried to pull herself together, when police sirens screamed through the night.

And they were coming closer. Coming for her and the others.

"Go," she told Shay. "This was our fight. We did what had to be done."

She hadn't agreed with Jon's decision to come to Tavern Red, but it didn't matter. They had faced off with Cain's men, had done what they could. She could live with it, even if she was one of the casualties.

Shay's gaze dropped to the blood on her hands, then to Cain's dead body. Dropping to his knees, he rifled through Cain's pockets, removing his wallet before turning his attention to the ring on Cain's finger.

"What are you doing?" Ava asked him.

"It will take them a while to identify him without this stuff," Shay explained. "Cain isn't someone who makes a point of having his fingerprints in the criminal database. It will buy us some time." He glanced back as the sound of sirens got louder, closer. "Listen to me, Ava. It doesn't have to be this way. It doesn't have to end like this."

"What are you talking about?" she said, already resigned to her fate at the hands of the police closing in on them.

"Do you trust me?" he asked her.

She hesitated, remembering those same words coming from his lips back at the shelter.

"Come on, Ava. If there's anyone you can trust, it should be me."

She couldn't argue the statement so she said nothing.

"You didn't finish your training," Shay continued, standing and stuffing Cain's personal effects in his own pocket. "That's why you made a mistake."

The sirens got louder, brasher, piercing through the approaching night as a fleet of police cars pulled into the alleyway, blocking them in on both sides.

"You killed the wrong man!" Shay shouted over the cacophony.

She tried to make sense of Shay's statement, her heart beating wildly as the police cars raced toward them, the outdated Sonoma County sedans piling into the alleyway, leaving no room for escape. They pinned Ava and Shay with their headlights. Ava held up her hands, shielding her eyes from the glare, and the cops leapt from their vehicles, pointing guns and yelling at them to keep their hands up, palms facing outward.

"Let me do the talking," Shay muttered as the police moved in.

"You should have let me die," Ava said under her breath.

"Please. You've got way too much work left to do."

Ava held still, her eyes falling to Cain's body at their feet. This did not look good. Not under any circumstances and definitely not combined with the carnage inside Tavern Red.

"That's all right, guys!" Shay called out. "I've got it under control!"

Ava allowed her eyes to shift to him, afraid to let the rest of her body follow. What the hell was he doing?

"Shay Thomas," he said, holding up a shimmering brass badge. "LAPD."

CHAPTER THIRTY-TWO

"Y OU'RE A COP?!" AVA EXCLAIMED UNDER HER breath.

She'd known he wasn't a bartender. Their history had told her that much. But she had no idea he was on the force.

The look he shot her told her everything she did need to know, which was basically to shut up.

He moved toward the cops, gesturing for them to join him by the back wall of Tavern Red. They conversed in hushed tones while Ava remained with her hands up, still afraid to move for fear of startling the one cop who still had his gun—and his eyes—on her.

Shay seemed like a different person in the company of the other officers. His posture was different, even the way he angled his head when he was talking to them. And their posture changed, too, as they ducked their heads a little, nodding in agreement. Ava had no idea who Shay was, but in less than ten minutes he'd become an authority figure to Sonoma law enforcement.

A couple of minutes later the men backed away, tucking their guns into their holsters as one of them returned to his car, grabbing the radio and requesting an ambulance.

Shay crossed the pavement, making his way back to Ava. "Let's go."

"Wait . . . What?" she said, still standing with her hands up. But Shay was already walking away. "What's going on?"

He walked back to her. "Do you want to get out of here or not?"

"I want to get out of here," she said, still confused.

"Then come on. I took care of things. For now."

"What does that mean?" she asked.

"Let's just say they might come knocking for an interview in a day or two, but I bought us some time."

She looked back at the police, already taping off the area around Cain's body. "Maybe I should just tell them my side of the story now . . ."

Shay tightened his grip on her arm. "Your friend that was taken. Do you care for him?"

Ava looked at Shay, unsure what he was getting at.

"Clearly you do or you wouldn't have run out here to help him."

"He's my friend. I . . ." She tried to figure out how to de-fine her feelings for Jon. "Well, I guess I . . ."

Shay ignored her stuttering. "If you want to find him, we need to get out of here. The police are going to be all over Tavern Red any minute."

He led her through the back door. Reena and Jane had wrapped Cruz in a blanket, but Reena still sat on the floor, holding his body and stroking his face. Tears streamed down her cheeks, her pale skin stained from crying.

Seeing them reenter the bar, Jane stood. "What's happened? I heard police . . . What's going on?"

"We need to get out of here," Shay said, striding into the room. "Now."

Jane looked around. "What about Jon?"

"They took him," Ava said, her throat still sore from Vic's assault on her neck.

"Who?"

"We don't know yet," Shay answered. "But the police are in the alley out back. I bought us some time, but I figure we've got five minutes, max, before they swarm this place. After that, none of us will get out of here for a long time."

Reena looked up at them. "Cain?"

"Dead," Ava said.

"Good." Reena's face hardened as she stood. "Now let's get the rest of those bastards."

"What would you like to do with Cruz?" he asked gently.

Reena blanched. "You know his name."

He sighed. "Yes."

She shook her head. "Who are you?"

"This is Shay Thomas," Ava explained. "He's the one who recruited me."

"But . . . what are you doing here?" asked Jane.

Shay rubbed a tired hand over his face. "Listen, I'd be happy to have this conversation later, but we really need to get out of here before the police decide they should check Tavern Red for witnesses to Cain's murder." He looked around at the unconscious bodies and broken furniture. "I think we can all agree that would be a bad thing."

Reena turned sad eyes on Cruz's body. "I know where to take him."

CHAPTER THIRTY-THREE

THEY HEADED TOWARD THE PACIFIC, SHAY DRIVING with Ava in the passenger seat. Jane sat with Reena, still cradling Cruz's body, in the back. Shay didn't start talking until they were clear of Tavern Red.

"I've been tending bar at Tavern Red for nearly six months," he explained.

But Ava had already started piecing it together. Shay couldn't go with her to Rebun Island because he'd been assigned to infiltrate Cain's organization.

"You said Cain was dead," Reena said from the back. "What happened?"

Shay explained how they had found Cain, lying in the alley already dead, and Vic's assault on Ava.

"Then the police came," explained Ava. "And that's where Shay has some more explaining to do."

"Why?" asked Jane.

He sighed. "Look, I was a cop, okay? In Los Angeles."

Ava studied his face, strong in the light of the dash. "What happened?"

He was silent a minute, following Reena's directions and getting on the highway.

"People think cops have so much power, but the truth is, they're about as powerless as you can get. Rules, paperwork, a chain of command that won't let you take a piss without a signature from your chief..." He shook his head. "I guess you could say I don't do well with rules. Especially when they mean not getting the bad guys or when half of those bad guys are other police officers. People who swore to protect and to serve."

"So you went to work for Takeda?" Ava asked.

He chuckled. "That's the short version."

She wanted to know the rest of it. Wanted to know how he'd come to know their sensei. But now wasn't the time. Reena was still grieving, holding her dead lover for the last time as they made their way to the ocean.

Ava realized something. "You were the one who told Takeda about the Starling Gala on May first."

"I knew a meeting was going down," Shay confirmed. "I was going to plant a recorder on Cain's jacket before the party."

"We screwed it up," Ava groaned. "Cain wasn't supposed to die. He was supposed to be our source for information inside the party."

Shay nodded. "There was going to be an exchange of information at the gala that would help you take down not only Cain, but Reinhardt, Charles Bay... everyone associated with what was done to you and the others."

"We never should have come here," Ava said.

"Doesn't matter now," Shay said. "We need to clean up the mess and move on."

"How do we do that?" Reena asked.

Shay reached around his seat belt, pulling a folded-up photograph from his pocket. He passed it to Ava.

"Darren Marcus used to do Cain's dirty work, back before he grew a conscience and went into hiding. Cain tried to stifle him. Permanently. But Marcus is a professional. Went off the grid. No one's been able to find him. Until now."

Ava looked at the photograph, studying the middle-aged man with the widow's peak and goatee before passing the picture to Reena in the backseat.

"Wells knows where he is but won't discuss it over the phone," Shay continued. "The meeting at Starling Vineyards is going to tell us where Marcus is hiding. And once Wells discloses his location, they'll set the dogs on him."

"Marcus is the last link to my mother's murder," Reena said softly, still looking at the picture. "He's the one who pulled the trigger."

"And if Wells kills him, he can't confess," Shay confirmed.

"So we need to find him before they do," Ava concluded.

"If Marcus is killed, we'll never be able to clear Simon Benton's name, will we?" Reena asked.

"And nothing will lead back to Reinhardt," Ava added. "Starling will remain in his filthy hands."

Their missions were even more entwined than Ava had thought, every wrong committed against them perpetrated by people who made a career out of doing it to others, too. Now, with Cruz dead, Jon missing, and their common enemies revealed, Ava felt more bonded to Reena and Jane than ever.

"What about me?" Jane asked. "What do I have to do with all of this?"

Shay took a deep breath. "Well, back when your—"

"Shay," Reena said in warning. "Don't."

Shay's surprise was written all over his face. "You haven't told her?"

Jane leaned forward as Shay pulled off the freeway. "Told me what?"

Everyone in the car grew silent.

"You know what?" Jane said angrily. "I'm sick of this. Sick of being kept in the dark. You expect me to run around, helping you guys out, without any explanation of how I'm connected to everything. Or anything."

Ava felt a pang of sympathy for her. As horrific as it was knowing what had been taken from her—and who had done it—it seemed even more harrowing to *not* know what had happened. To not know what you had lost. To not even remember who you were.

"Tell me how you know me, Shay. Please," Jane pleaded.

Shay only hesitated a moment. "I was there the day Takeda brought you to Rebun Island. And I know who you really are."

CHAPTER THIRTY-FOUR

"DON'T DO THIS, SHAY," REENA SAID.

Jane glared at her, hurt warring with anger. Reena was one of the very few people she counted on. She hadn't really gotten to know Ava, and Cruz had always been, well ... Cruz. But Reena was consistently able to calm her with a laugh or a chat.

Now, just like everyone else, Reena wanted to keep Jane's past a secret.

"Why are you doing this to me?" Jane asked. "I thought you were my friend."

"I am your friend," Reena said gently. "That's why I'm doing it."

Something in Reena's eyes got Jane's attention. Some kind of secret knowledge that hinted at the truth. All at once, Jane understood.

"There was a file on me, wasn't there?" she asked softly.

Reena took a deep breath. "There was, okay? But I didn't read it. I didn't think it would be right."

Anger roared through Jane's head like a freight train. "Don't you think *I* deserve to read it? That I deserve to know who I am before I risk my life with the rest of you?"

"Takeda said—"

Jane interrupted her, letting out a bitter laugh. "You're going to use Takeda's rules as an excuse? That's funny coming from someone who was willing to defy him to suit your own needs. Hypocrite, much?"

Reena looked down at Cruz, the streetlights passing intermittently over his still face. "I'm just trying to protect you."

"That's not your job. Or your decision."

Reena turned to her with an expression of regret. "Look, I caught a glimpse of your folder, before I realized it was yours. And yes, I saw Reinhardt's and Wells's photos in there. But that's all I saw before I closed it, I swear."

"Where is it, Reena?" Jane said from between clenched teeth. "Where's my file?"

Reena hesitated. "I'm sorry. I left it in Japan."

Jane turned to the window, her heart sinking. "So everyone gets to know their path to revenge but me."

"Listen," Ava said from the front seat, "you need to put this aside for now. It's not going to help us get the guys who did this to us, who killed Cruz, who took Jon. We need to focus on the mission."

They grew silent. Ava was right. What was done was done. Jane's file was in Japan, and as pissed as she was at Reena for leaving it there, there was nothing to be done about it now.

She looked at Shay, giving it one last try. "What about you?"

He shook his head. "I have to trust Takeda on this. He's more than my boss; he's my mentor. And he's yours, too. What's the point in having a mentor if you don't trust that he knows what he's doing?"

"So what's the plan?" Reena asked, obviously trying to

change the subject. "How are we going to get a recorder into the meeting between Reinhardt and Wells now that Cain is dead?"

Ava turned around in her seat, meeting Reena's eyes. "We won't. We'll plant you in there instead."

"What are you talking about?" Reena asked.

"Yeah, Ava," Shay chimed in. "What *are* you talking about?"

"Marie told me that Reinhardt always hires a girl to be his date at these kinds of parties," Ava explained. "Reena can be that girl."

Reena thought about it. "What if he recognizes me?" she asked. "Cain did."

"Barely," says Ava. "You've been out of the spotlight for a long time. Your mother's death, your training in Japan . . . it's changed you. It's changed all of us. And not just in appearance, either."

"She's right," Shay said. "And we can set you up with a disguise, too, just to be safe."

"Fine," Reena agreed. "Plant me in the room with Reinhardt and Wells."

"Perfect." Shay's expression was a little too self-satisfied.

"Now what are you hiding?" Jane asked, annoyance creeping into her voice.

"Let's just say Reena isn't the only thing we're going to plant in that meeting."

Jane didn't bother asking what he meant. What was the point? Shay was disseminating information on a need-to-know basis.

And no one thought Jane needed to know anything.

CHAPTER THIRTY-FIVE

T HEY PULLED INTO A SMALL, ROCKY INLET COM-
posed of the gritty Pacific coastline and a large, sand-covered
jetty. Reena's gaze came to rest on a battered sign.

WELCOME TO BODEGA BAY.

Shay parked Marie's car and turned off the engine. They
sat without talking, the ticking of the cooling engine their only
company.

Reena looked down, wanting to memorize the strong planes
of Cruz's face, the lips that had kissed her so tenderly. Wanting
to tattoo it in her mind like the circle that branded the back of
her neck. She touched his hands, cool and dry. The hands that
had held hers when she'd been all alone in the world.

Finally, she couldn't put it off any longer.

"I'm going to need some help."

Shay got out of the car and walked around to Reena's side.
He opened the door, easing Cruz's body off Reena's lap, lifting the other man into his arms like a sleeping child.

"This is where Cruz and Simon used to come when things
got rough at home," she explained as they made their way to the

water's edge. "Cruz told me they called their trips here 'adventures.'"

Ava touched her arm. "It sounds like the perfect place," she said softly.

Reena nodded. It was the only place she could think of. A place of love and hope. A place Simon could come to be near his brother when they finally cleared his name.

And they would clear his name. For Cruz.

She stepped closer to Shay, but looked closely at Cruz's face.

"I don't know how I'll go on without you, but I will, because that's how you'd want it." She laughed softly, tears streaming down her face. "I can almost hear you now, telling me to move my ass." She placed a tender kiss on his lips. "Good night, my love. Sleep well."

She stepped back, nodding to Shay, who walked into the surf and gently placed Cruz's body into the rough waters. The sweeping tide brushed her feet, as if trying to comfort her as the water wrapped its arms around Cruz, pulling him out to sea.

She watched the water until she was sure he was gone. Then she turned to the others.

"I can't let him die for nothing."

Ava shook her head. "We won't."

Shay stared out over the water, the moon casting a column of light on its surface. "The most powerful hunter on the planet isn't the lion or the tiger. It's not even a cheetah or a bird of prey." He looked at Reena. At all of them. "It's a pack of wild African painted dogs. Fierce, violent, calculating. On their own, they don't amount to much. But when they work together, their rate of takedown is incomparable."

Takeda had been right. Emotions got in the way of revenge. Cruz would still be there if he hadn't loved Reena enough to die for her. Reena wouldn't feel like the life had been sucked out of her if she hadn't loved Cruz.

And now Reena understood something else. Retribution wasn't just a willingness to send people to hell. It was a willingness to go there with them to see the job done. She knew it firsthand, because if there was a hell, this had to be it.

"C'mon," Shay said, turning away from the water. "Time to fly."

Reena looked one last time at the water, the tide ebbing and flowing. She imagined Cruz, drifting on the swells, part of the sea now. Part of everything. She would come back when she'd cleared Simon's name, she decided. When she'd avenged Cruz's death. She would come back and sit on the rocks and tell Cruz everything she'd never had the courage to say.

She was surprised to feel someone grab her hand.

Ava.

And then, a soft grip on her other one.

Jane.

They stood there for a moment, hand in hand.

"What do we do now?" Reena finally asked.

Ava took a deep breath. "We adapt."

CHAPTER THIRTY-SIX

"Fore!" CHARLIE CALLED OUT, ROCKING A NINE-iron, his backswing in perfect form.

The weather was perfect, a mélange of color brought to life under a clear blue sky, the Heritage Hollows golf course set against scenic hillsides and emerald-colored fields. Even with his sunglasses, Charlie had to squint against the sun, watching as his shot blasted the bunker, sending a spray of sand onto the green.

"You're going to have to do better than that," William Reinhardt sneered.

He picked up Charlie's ball, knocking it against his golf shoes.

"It's just a game," Charlie said, stifling a rush of annoyance.

Reinhardt didn't grace the comment with a response. Charlie knew all too well that nothing was just a game for Reinhardt. Not even a game.

Reinhardt glanced down at his Ulysse Nardin wristwatch. "I'd show you how it's done—again—but it's time to head back."

They walked back to the car and made their way to Starling. Charlie wasn't surprised to see that the guest lot was full as they pulled onto the grounds of the elaborate estate. Starling's tasting rooms were ripe with visitors year-round, but as spring turned to summer, Napa was a hotbed of activity.

And Starling was the region's star.

Reinhardt and Charlie were greeted with a mixture of awe and reverence as they made their way across the estate. William had purchased the vineyard from Ava Winters after the death of her grandmother. At least that's how it was perceived.

And Charlie was his right-hand man.

Many of the locals were relieved when Reinhardt took over. True, he wasn't born and raised in Napa, but rumors had swirled for months that the Winters girl was running the vineyard into the ground; Starling was on the verge of bankruptcy. If it weren't for Reinhardt, it might not be in business at all, and while his business dealings since coming to Napa had proven suspect, he was undeniably powerful. That left the locals only two choices: oppose him or befriend him.

And opposing him was dangerous.

Reinhardt and Charlie entered the main house through two large plank and batten doors. They passed through the cathedral-like foyer, shoes clicking on pristine marble, and went straight for the study. Reinhardt headed for the bar, pouring himself a glass of Barbera wine and surveying its deep ruby hue before taking a sip.

Pouring a glass for himself, Charlie took a whiff, noting the subtle cherry aroma. He took a drink, looking through the study doors to the grand staircase. He'd been at Starling countless times since Reinhardt bought it.

Since Reinhardt stole it with Charlie's help.

But Charlie never stopped looking at the wall next to the stairs, his gaze going right to the empty space where the portrait of Ava, her mother, and her grandmother had once hung.

Charlie sometimes felt sick when he thought about it. About what he put Ava through so he could afford the Italian loafers on his feet. He liked his new life. Liked the luxury and security of it. But still the question of whether he'd do it again moved through his mind like a swinging pendulum, steady and constant.

"Drink up, Charles," Reinhardt said, eyeing Charlie's still-full glass. "And relax. Tonight will be enjoyable, even if we do have to put up with Wells."

"The senator?" Charlie asked. "I didn't realize he was on the guest list."

Reinhardt waved off the statement. "You know how politicians are, always trying to see and be seen."

Reinhardt wasn't telling him everything. Charlie could hear it in the too-flip tone of his voice, a dead giveaway from a man who was never truly flip about anything. They were partners of a sort, but Charlie was nothing if not honest with himself.

Honor among thieves was only nice—or even possible—in theory.

"I'm going to change," Reinhardt said, setting his empty glass on the bar and heading for the staircase. He was halfway there when he turned back to Charlie. "By the way, why is the Starling Gala on May first? I've always wondered about it."

Charlie kept his face impassive. Reinhardt wasn't the only one with secrets.

"No clue."

Ava blows out the candles on the enormous pink cake as Charlie films the scene with a handheld video camera. The small gathering in the Starling Vineyards atrium—Sylvie, Marie, Marie's daughter, Daniella, and a handful of Starling employees—applauds Ava on her twenty-first birthday.

"You shouldn't have," Ava says with a laugh, her black crepe dress setting off her green eyes.

"Once you taste that cake, you'll be glad we did," Charlie says. "I tested it myself when we were trying to decide which one to order."

Ava gazes lovingly at him as Sylvie wraps him in an embrace, relieved that Ava has someone she can trust in her life. Sylvie is increasingly aware that she won't live forever, and without Ava's parents, the girl will need the support of others when Sylvie's gone.

Everyone raises a glass of prized Zinfandel. Sylvie coughs a bit as she drinks, startling her granddaughter.

"Grandmother? Are you all right?" Ava asks, setting down her glass and hurrying over to her.

"Daniella, go get Sylvie some water," Marie orders her daughter.

Daniella hurries to the kitchen but is stopped by Sylvie.

"That won't be necessary," Sylvie rasps. "I'm perfectly fine. I just want to enjoy the party."

Sylvie catches the concern in Ava's eyes. It's true that she's been under the weather of late, but she's as tough as they come. Napa's summer heat is on its way. She'll be right as rain in no time at all.

She raises her glass. "To Ava," she says. "And to the Starling Gala."

The chorus is repeated by the group.

Charlie leans in to Sylvie as everyone drinks. "Is it a coincidence," he asks, "that the gala is the same day as Ava's birthday?"

"Not at all. Ava's mother planned it this way." She takes his arm. "Someday when we're all gone Ava's great-great-grandkids—and who knows, Charlie, maybe they'll be yours, too"—she winks at him—"will still be celebrating Ava's birthday, even if they don't know it. Because people, dear, they come and go. Some faster than others, some with more impact. But tradition can't be so easily quelled."

Charlie is touched in spite of himself. Later, while the women dress for the gala, Charlie wanders the house, taking in the classic simplicity of its furnishings, the fine art and antiques collected over more than one lifetime. It's a brand of grandeur that can't be bought. Reinhardt might one day own the place. Might even live here. But it won't be the same without the people who built and nurtured it.

He's just come down the main hallway, past the grand staircase, when he feels someone watching him. Turning, his gaze falls on the painting of Ava, her mother, and Sylvie on the wall. The women seem to watch him, their eyes vibrant and alive even on canvas. They are beautiful, their fine bone structure and regal bearing echoing across the generations.

He stands there a moment, feeling the weight of their legacy. It's an uncomfortable burden, especially under the circumstances, and a moment later he turns to go, trying to ignore the feeling that they are watching him every step of the way.

CHAPTER THIRTY-SEVEN

"HOW ARE YOU FEELING?" AVA ASKED AS THE MORN-
ing sun slanted across the bed.

Reena hadn't wanted to be alone when they returned
from Bodega Bay the night before. They had fallen asleep on
Ava's bed without speaking about Cruz's death or anything
that had happened at Tavern Red.

"I don't know," Reena said softly. "I can't feel anything."

Ava didn't try to comfort her. Didn't say any of the trite
things people say in these situations. It didn't help. It only
turned the tables, forcing the grieving to comfort everyone
else in their desperation to say the right thing.

Ava knew it all firsthand.

Reena got out of bed and moved toward the bathroom.

"Can I do anything for you?" Ava asked. "Get anything
for you?"

She hesitated. "Yeah, you can help me get Wells and Reinhardt."

She closed the bathroom door, and a minute later Ava
heard the water running in the shower.

She lay there, thinking about Reena, about how much her

world had changed in just a few short hours. It wasn't a surprise. Nothing was certain.

Nothing.

She got up and walked to the window, looking out over Marie's field. She wondered about Jon. What was he seeing this morning? Was he even still alive? Could he be on the run because he'd killed Cain?

But instinct said that Jon had been taken by some of Cain's men. She'd thought they got them all inside Tavern Red, but it was possible some of them had been in the back when all hell broke loose. And if Cain's men had Jon, what incentive would they have for keeping him alive? He could already be dead.

She shook her head and turned in to the empty room. There was no point thinking about it. The only thing they could do for Jon was to get ahold of Wells and Reinhardt, force them to explain what they'd done with him before they paid for all their other crimes.

The smell of sugar and browning butter crept under the door. Coffee and pastries wouldn't change anything for Reena, but it might make it a little easier to face the day.

Ava opened the door, planning to bring a tray up for Reena, and nearly crashed into a shirtless Shay.

"Whoa!" she said, taking a reflexive step backward.

"Whoa yourself," he grinned, clad only in jeans. "Thought you two could use some breakfast."

She dropped her eyes to the tray in his hand, laden with pastries and two steaming mugs. "Wow . . . thanks. You didn't have to do that."

"It's not a big deal," he said. "You know, I just got up,

whipped up these delicious croissants, ground some coffee beans . . ."

She smacked his arm playfully, careful not to upset the tray. "Yeah, right."

"Want some company?" he asked.

She stepped back, opening the door wider. "Sure. Reena's in the shower."

She took the tray to the bed and sat down, picking up one of the buttery croissants as Shay pulled the desk chair around to face her.

"Want one?" Ava indicated the tray.

He shook his head. "Already ate."

"What about Jane?" Ava asked. "She still pissed?"

"I'd say that's a safe bet." He glanced at the closed bathroom door. "How is she?"

Ava took a drink of hot coffee, savoring the smoky bitterness. "Devastated. Numb. Still in shock, I think."

They sat in companionable silence while Ava ate. When she'd polished off a second pastry and half the coffee, she brushed off her hands.

"So what's up? The breakfast was sweet, but I have a feeling you didn't come up here to practice your room service skills."

"It's time to get to work," Shay said simply.

They turned to the door as Jane walked in. She crossed the room and sat on the bed next to Ava. "So let's work."

Shay surveyed her silently. Ava didn't think it was her imagination that she saw affection in his eyes. Whatever had happened on Rebun Island when Jane had first arrived, whatever

Shay knew, he cared about her. It was obvious to Ava even if Jane was too blinded by her own anger to see it.

The bathroom door opened

"Reena, Shay came—"

Ava tried to warn her, but it was too late. Reena stepped into the room, wrapped in a towel. Water droplets traced a line from her jaw to her collarbone.

"Jesus, Shay!" she said when she saw him. "Turn around."

"Don't worry," he said calmly. "I've been trained not to care."

"That's what they all say," Reena said. "Now turn around."

He faced the wall, smirking.

Reena shot a glance at Ava. "Thanks for the warning."

"Sorry," Ava said.

Reena grabbed a T-shirt and pair of jeans and hurried back into the bathroom. She emerged fully dressed a minute later, picking the still-full coffee cup off the tray.

She took a drink. "Okay. Let's do this."

Shay looked at them. "You're not going to like what I have to say."

"I don't like a lot of things," Reena said. "Say it."

"You—all of you—created this mess. You didn't follow orders. You left before you were ready. And now Cruz is dead and Jon is missing." Reena flinched, but she didn't say anything as Shay continued. "Despite all of that, this task must be accomplished. Your revenge paths all lead back to the three men who took everything from you. One is dead. The other two are still out there."

Ava could add one more name to that list: Charlie.

"Just tell me one thing," Jane said. "Did these three men put me in the condition I'm in?"

Shay hesitated before nodding.

"Why?" Her voice was forlorn.

Shay stood, coming to stand next to her. He brushed the hair from her face, a surprisingly intimate gesture that made his feelings for her obvious.

"Because they felt they had to."

CHAPTER THIRTY-EIGHT

REINHARDT DIPPED HIS HAND IN THE MARBLE fountain, skimming the water's surface. The marble was smooth and white, as unique as the clouds that line Napa's afternoon skyline. Scooping out some of the change shimmering at the bottom of the fountain, he studied a rare silver dollar among the other change.

Someone had a very ambitious wish.

Something caught his eye at the base of the fountain, near a small, subtle crack. He leaned in, rubbing his fingertips over something engraved in the hard stone: R3.

It didn't mean anything to him, but just below it were the words of Henry Wadsworth Longfellow: *"That which the fountain sends forth returns again to the fountain."*

He contemplated its meaning, its context as his eyes dropped to yet another inscription.

"To Sylvie . . ."

The name brought with it a memory of the elegant old woman, having brunch with her granddaughter at the club. Ironic that she would be immortalized on what was now Reinhardt's property.

His reflection in the water caught him off guard. The lines under his eyes were thicker, the creases in his forehead deeper. He consoled himself with the adage that with age comes wisdom, priding himself on plenty of the latter.

In fact, he'd do it all over again if given the chance.

"From such a gentle thing, from such a fountain of all delight, my every pain is born."

He turned to see Charlie walking toward him, dressed in a sleek black tux, tie loose around his neck, and a diamond-studded accessory named Bo on his arm.

"Michelangelo's words, not mine," Charlie said. "Still, they're oddly fitting, wouldn't you say?"

Reinhardt stood. "Not at all. I feel no pain. Neither should you. And if you do, keep it to yourself. That wasn't part of the deal."

Charlie glanced at the coin in Reinhardt's hand. "If you need me to spot you a few bucks, all you have to do is ask," Charlie joked.

Reinhardt flicked the coin back into the fountain, causing a small splash. "Just contemplating the uselessness of this fountain. There's more value in the coins tossed in the water than in the foolhardy wishes people make. This thing's an eyesore. Maybe I'll have it removed."

"It gives people hope, no?" Bo said with a thick Scandinavian accent.

He leveled his gaze at her. "Hope is handing over the reins of one's life to a fate that doesn't exist."

Charlie kissed Bo's cheek. "Go on in. I'll meet you in the atrium for a drink."

Reinhardt watched her departure, Bo's snug cocktail dress hugging every one of her considerable curves.

"The fountain was installed for Sylvie to honor her work with the Relief/Recover/Rebuild Foundation," Charlie explained.

"Like I said, an eyesore, just like the old bat herself," Reinhardt said. He looked at Charlie, a mean shine in his eye. "But if you like it, perhaps I'll have you removed as well, although your friend, Bo, can stay."

"She's not your type," Charlie said. "I didn't pay for her."

"What's the point in that?" Reinhardt asked. "If you don't pay, you don't always get what you want."

"Ever just want someone to keep you company?" Charlie asked.

"No," Reinhardt said simply.

They stood there in the late afternoon heat, staring each other down. Reinhardt couldn't recall when their camaraderie turned to animosity. When they became adversaries instead of allies. Was it after Reinhardt bought the estate? After the Winters girl left town? Probably. Charlie always did have a soft spot for her, although he would never admit it at the time.

"There was a fellow named Count Victor Lustig, Charlie. Are you familiar with him?" Reinhardt asked.

"One of the greatest con men in history," Charlie said. "Pretended to work for the French government and sold the Eiffel Tower. Twice. He even had the gall to con Al Capone."

Reinhardt looked Charlie in the eye. "A well-known quote from Lustig—and pardon my missteps with it, I'm paraphrasing—goes, 'Everything turns gray when I don't have at least one mark on the horizon. Life then seems empty and depressing. I cannot understand honest men. They lead desperate lives—'"

"'—full of boredom,'" Charlie finished.

"Why are you still here, Charles?" Reinhardt asked. "You clearly have mixed feelings about our spoils. Perhaps a new mark is in order."

Charlie looked down at his reflection in the water. "I don't think that's who I am anymore."

Reinhardt knew it for the lie it was. Man couldn't deny his true nature. Not really.

He stood, slapping Charlie on the back. "Nonsense. We're one and the same. I just have the courage to be honest about it."

CHAPTER THIRTY-NINE

A VA STOOD ON THE PORCH, BREATHING IN THE dry Napa air and gazing at the golden fields stretching into the distance. It was hard to believe that only two days before, she was standing in this exact spot with Jon, the moon bright and swollen as he kissed her. Like so many things, she wished she could have the moment back.

"There you are," a voice said behind her.

Ava turned to see Marie with Daniella, carrying a large pink cake with a single candle burning at its center. Shay, Reena, and Jane stood smiling behind them. They began to sing, the notes of "Happy Birthday" ringing through the porch's wooden rafters, traveling out across the fields.

"What . . . ?" Ava began. She shook her head as the song came to a close. "I can't believe you remembered."

"Of course," Marie said, surprised. "Why wouldn't we?"

Ava wiped a tear from her cheek. "Because I didn't."

She had been so consumed with thoughts and plans for the gala, for finally coming face-to-face with the people who had ruined her, that she had forgotten the gala also marked another occasion: her birthday.

"I can't believe you guys did this," Ava said.

"I had Daniella order the cake," Marie said. "I remembered that it was your favorite."

Ava smiled, first at Marie and then at Daniella. "Thank you. Really."

Daniella smiled shyly.

"Well, what are you waiting for?" Shay asked her. "Make a wish."

Ava looked at the cake, the candle dripping wax on the pink fondant, and closed her eyes. She thought of everything she'd lost. Everything she suffered. Then she wished. Not just to get it back, but to make those who had taken it pay.

She blew out the candle and Marie and Daniella sliced thick pieces of cake and passed them around.

Ava stood in the circle of friends new and old, laughing as Marie and Daniella regaled the others with stories of her past birthdays. She was surprised to find that remembering didn't hurt as much as it once had, her pain dulled by the knowledge that she was closer than ever to making those responsible for it pay.

Later that night, she was upstairs when a knock sounded on the bedroom door.

"Shay," she said when she opened the door to find him there. Her gaze dropped to the large gift box in his hands. "What's that?"

"Let's just call it a birthday gift from Takeda."

"Takeda?" Even in the throes of revenge, the name seemed pulled from another life, another time. She had a flash of Rebun Island's rocky cliffs, the briny air of the sea rising on the fog off the channel. "How does he . . . ?"

Shay raised an eyebrow, handing her the box. "You didn't really think he was unaware of your whereabouts?"

She shook her head, realizing that the notion was foolish. Takeda knew everything.

"Should I open it now?" Ava asked, taking it to her bed.

Shay followed her into the room. "That's the idea."

She sat down, laying the package on the bed. The box was huge. She peeled back the crisp white wrapping paper and lifted off the lid, digging through mounds of tissue paper to a shimmer of violet silk.

She lifted it from the box, stunned silent as a simple, violet sheath dress was revealed.

"I don't understand," she said, looking at Shay.

"Takeda thought you might be out of place at the Starling Gala wearing a karate *gi*."

"He knows we're going," she said. It wasn't a question.

Shay nodded. "I know it's your birthday, but Jane and Reena got dresses, too."

Ava felt an unexpected rush of shame at the thought of Takeda. "Does he know what happened at Tavern Red?"

Shay leveled his gaze at her. "Ava."

"Right." She nodded. "He knows everything. I keep forgetting."

"You'd do well to stop forgetting." He stood to go. "Takeda forgets nothing, and while he offers you his support, you won't ever be allowed back at Rebun Island unless you and the others succeed tonight."

Ava's heart sank. She wasn't even aware that she wanted to go back to Rebun to finish her training. The realization gave her a fresh round of determination.

"What will I be doing while Reena infiltrates the meeting between Wells and Reinhardt?"

Shay reached into his jacket and removed a manila envelope.

"What's this?" Ava asked, taking it.

"A taste of what following orders feels like."

CHAPTER FORTY

THEY CHANGED IN THE BATHROOM OF A LOCAL HO-tel, not wanting to draw attention to their plans. It was kind of Marie to offer them shelter—especially since they had little money with which to pay her—but they couldn't risk putting her and Daniella on Reinhardt's radar.

Shay waited in the lobby while the women donned the designer dresses Takeda had sent, each of them somehow perfect for the woman who wore it. Takeda's knowledge clearly extended beyond linguistics and fencing.

Reena was dazzling in white, the dress short enough to show off her mile-long legs. Her red hair was a fiery contrast to the dress's purity, its cap sleeves demure against a plunging neckline.

"You look amazing," Ava said.

The violet dress was even more beautiful on than it had been in the box, drawing attention to her curves while main-taining the classic brand of elegance that was a birthright of the Winters name. Ava wondered if Takeda had chosen the color as an homage to the wine that was her family's legacy.

"You both look amazing," Jane said, admiring her own reflection and the mauve lace shift Takeda had sent her.

By the time they arrived outside the estate, night had descended upon the terroir. Reena and Ava left Shay and Jane in Marie's car, parked in the shadows of a side road rarely used by anyone but the field hands.

"Wish us luck," Ava said, lifting her gown as she exited the car.

"Good luck," Shay said.

Jane was silent, brooding on her lack of a clear role in the night's events. Ava sympathized, but even she didn't know everything thanks to Shay's now infamously locked lips.

Moving across the long grass, Reena and Ava hurried down the steep hill that was the backbone of the estate. They glided past rows of grapes topped with netting to ward off preying birds. It was all strangely familiar, the rich smell of the crops guiding her home.

Reena didn't regard the scent with quite so much affection.

"What the hell is that stink?" she muttered. "It's rank."

Ava chuckled softly in the dark. "Fertilizer, ripening grapes . . . it's the smell of a vineyard."

"Well, it sucks," Reena said, cursing as her heel caught on one of the vines.

"This way," Ava said, leading Reena through a steep ravine that took them closer to the estate.

In the distance, Lake Berryessa sparkled in the moonlight, its shine granting them a little extra light as they traveled under the dark umbrella of the Petit Verdot grapes that grew at the edge of the vineyard.

Finally, they reached the back of the main house. They stood in the shelter of the vines for a couple of minutes, scanning the property for anyone who might be witness to their arrival.

When the coast was clear, they hurried across the open ground to the back terrace. But instead of stepping onto it, Ava navigated around and under it, scanning the ground.

"Damn it," she cursed. "Where the hell is it?"

"What are we looking for?" Reena asked.

"The door," Ava said.

"On the ground?" Reena looked down, shuffling over the dirt at their feet, a faint echo sounding under her heels. "I don't see anything."

"That's because you're standing on it." Ava waved her away. "Move over."

She brushed aside the overgrown weeds near Reena's feet to reveal a partially rusted door that even Sylvie hadn't known about. Reena bent down to help her, both of them tugging on the metal handle until the door opened with a quiet creak.

Ava brushed off her hands, glancing at Reena. "Follow me. And close the door behind you."

She stepped onto the first wooden tread and made her way into the darkness below them.

"You okay?" she called up to Reena, hearing the hesitancy in her descent.

"Yeah," Reena said. "I just . . . I can't see anything."

Ava reached back, taking Reena's hand. "It's okay. Just follow me."

A moment later, Reena's voice cut through the darkness. "I'm sorry, Ava."

Ava continued down the steps without looking back. "For what?"

"For acting the way I did when you first came to Rebun. I don't know why I was such a bitch."

Finally reaching the last step, Ava stepped onto the hard-packed cellar floor. "I understand. In fact, it would have been easier if it had stayed that way."

"How would that make things easier?" Reena asked, reaching the end of the staircase.

Ava pulled the string of a dusty lightbulb on the low-hanging ceiling. "Because then we wouldn't care what happens to each other tonight."

The light flickered briefly before fully illuminating the space. The room was just as Ava remembered. A hidden gem beneath the grandeur of the main house, the ceilings were lined with redwood, the mahogany walls polished to a deep, rich shine.

"Where are we? What is this?" Reena asked.

"It was an old, unused storage room that I decided to restore after my grandmother passed. I needed a project. Something to keep me busy. It felt good to breathe life into something new. Although I guess that doesn't make much sense."

Reena met her eyes. "Sure it does."

Ava looked around, the room a reminder of all she'd once planned. She wanted to expand her family's legacy, but she had made all the wrong choices.

"I really screwed things up," she said softly.

"Don't even go there," Reena advised. "That's how people

like Charlie and Reinhardt thrive—by making everyone else the scapegoat for their actions. They did this. Not you."

Ava nodded, trying to believe it.

She set down her sequined clutch, the envelope Shay had given her sticking out of the top, next to a 1977 Pinot Noir. It was the year her parents got married. She smiled, taking it as a good omen.

"What's that?" Reena asked, tipping her head at the manila envelope.

"A reason to believe in Takeda. That his training pays off and that we need to return to it when we're done here."

Reena grinned. "What does he have on Charlie?"

"Let's just say that if Charlie is at all capable of regret, this will be enough to send him into a tornado of it."

"And with what I'll be doing to him upstairs . . . ," Reena began.

"Good-bye, Charlie."

They traded steely looks, their shared resolve further bonding them.

"Let me check your makeup," Ava said, pulling Reena under the lightbulb.

Ava adjusted Reena's short platinum blonde wig, a perfect match to the choker around her neck. Tipping her head, Ava checked her smoky eyes for smudges and studied the prosthetic nose Shay had applied using spirit gum adhesive. She had been surprised when he'd gone to work, although she shouldn't have been.

Apparently there was no limit to the expertise imparted under Takeda's tutelage.

"Looks good," Ava said.

Reena shifted nervously on her feet, all traces gone of the cool, collected woman Ava first met on Rebun Island.

Ava leaned in to give her a hug. "You're going to do great."

Reena nodded, taking a deep breath. "How will we find Reinhardt's hired girl?"

Ava brushed some dust off her hands. "Don't worry. I'll make an entrance and pick her out."

"An entrance?" Reena asked. "You're not playing it low-key?"

"This is Napa. A grand entrance is the only kind that counts." Ava's face was grim. "Besides, if all eyes are on me, no one will be staring at you."

Motioning for Ava to turn around, Reena smoothed out the wrinkles in Ava's dress.

Ava checked her watch. "It's a quarter past eight. They're meeting at ten. Let's do this."

They exchanged a look. Sisters by fire.

They were crossing the cellar, moving to the staircase that would lead them up to the upper levels of the house, when something caught Ava's eye. She moved toward it, wondering if her eyes were deceiving her. But as she got closer, she knew she was right.

Cobwebs crisscrossed the gilded frame. Ava reached down, brushing them away, and came face-to-face with her mother and grandmother. And not just them. She was there, too. All three of them staring back from the painting that had hung on the wall by the staircase for as long as Ava remembered.

Her breath caught in her throat. She had assumed the painting was destroyed or sold. She had grieved its loss. But even greater than her surprise at its survival was her shock at its location.

Only Charlie knew about her renovation project.

Why would he save the painting?

She walked away, rattled and confused.

"Do you get sad, being here?" Reena asked softly.

Ava thought about it. "Not anymore. Now I just get angry."

She was on the staircase leading to the house when she realized Reena was still on the cellar floor.

"Is something wrong?" she asked.

Reena shook her head. "I'm just . . ." She laughed a little. "Well, I'm not even sure I know what it feels like, but I guess I'm scared." She hesitated. "And it creeps me out to think of sidling up to that bastard, Reinhardt, when Cruz—"

Ava walked back down the stairs. "Listen to me. You can do this. For your mother. For Cruz. For Simon, alone in a prison cell, petrified and desperate. You're not betraying Cruz. You're continuing his mission. And by doing that, you're keeping him alive."

Reena took a deep breath and put her hand on Ava's shoulder. "I'm ready."

They ascended the stairs leading to the estate. Ava opened a door at the top, pushing aside a small rolling shelf unit inside a large pantry. Reena stopped behind her as Ava slid open the pantry doors to reveal a sliver of the main kitchen.

Waiters and waitresses moved frantically about, too busy to notice the two women slip from the pantry and head for the corridor. Continuing down the main hall, they approached the big wooden doors that would take them to the party, in full swing in the tasting room.

"I hope no one recognizes me," Reena said as Ava reached for the door.

"Don't worry," Ava said. "They'll all be looking at me anyway."

CHAPTER FORTY-ONE

SHE'D BEEN EXPECTING HIM, BUT THE SIGHT OF Charlie roaming the tasting room still felt like a harsh slap in the face.

A tall, voluptuous blonde graced his arm as he laughed with the guests, patting them on the back and listening intently when they spoke to him. Like they were the only people in the room. In the world.

Ava knew that look, that feeling, all too well.

The Sangiovese flowed freely as men in Armani tuxedos stood next to women in designer dresses and Jimmy Choo stilettos. Ava and Reena waited for Charlie to move into the adjoining room before entering the party. Ava braced herself as the guests swiveled their collective heads, eyes coming to rest on her.

A murmur rolled through the crowd like a tidal wave, picking up speed as everyone realized who stood before them.

"Oh, God," Ava whispered to Reena. "All eyes on me."

"It's what we need to make everything else happen," Reena reminded her.

"Well, you're the media darling," Ava said. "What do I do?"

Reena flashed a smile bright enough to light the room. "Smile."

Ava walked farther into the room, head held high, as everyone continued their conversations, albeit with one eye on her.

"So," Reena said, looking around. "Which one is she?"

Ava scoped out the candidates. A beautiful woman sipped sherry over by a vintage café table. She wore a custom-tailored dress with a diamond necklace Ava pegged as real.

Not her.

Over by the fireplace, two dark-haired girls in faux-fur and hoop earrings laughed as a couple of sweater-vest-wearing sycophants in black-rimmed glasses did their best to keep the ladies entertained.

Interesting. But definitely not the kind of high-end prostitute hired by someone like Reinhardt.

"How about her?" Reena indicated an hourglass-shaped woman with crossed legs and a nest of black hair, face tipped to her phone as her fingers flew across the keys.

But Ava shook her head, motioning to the other side of the room where a tall, buxom woman with red hair surveyed the crowd, her fascination obvious. Her dress was just a little too low-cut, a rose pinned to one of the spaghetti straps.

"It's her," Ava said.

Reena seemed surprised. "How do you know?"

"A Napa socialite wouldn't be so curious. This kind of party is old hat up here. Plus, the lip gloss is a little too thick, the dress a little too—"

"Got it," Reena said with a chuckle. "So you're sure?"

She tipped her head at the woman. "Look for yourself."

The woman was openly studying the décor, running her hand over a gold-plated wine opener hanging on the wall. Ava remembered it, a gift from the OIV during a particularly rewarding year that saw Ava and her grandmother on the cover of Napa Valley's regional wine magazine. Starling's Cabernet had blown the competition out of the water at the Concours Mondial de Bruxelles international wine festival.

"Okay, then," Reena said, taking a deep breath.

"You can do this," Ava said.

She watched as Reena stood a little straighter, her manner changing from reserved wallflower to sultry seductress as she sashayed toward the copper-haired girl-for-hire.

A moment later, someone tapped Ava's shoulder.

She turned, nearly swallowing her own tongue as she came face-to-face with Charlie.

All the preparation in the world hadn't prepared her for the shock of seeing him, of being so close to him. She was caught in the net of his cologne, a scent he'd been wearing since the day she met him. A montage of memory flashed through her mind. Their first kiss. The first time they made love.

But it only took a second to remember how it all ended.

"Ava," he breathed, his face white with shock.

She forced a placid expression on her face, surprised when the rest of her body followed. Tranquility flowed through her as she looked at his face. Finally. *Finally.*

"So then you remember," she said.

"Remember? Of course I remember," he said, smiling nervously. "But what are you doing here?"

"The expression is 'you can't go home again,' right?" she said. "I guess I wanted to find out for myself."

He narrowed his eyes. "What do you really want, Ava?"

She smiled, grabbing his hand and pulling him to the center of the room. "To dance."

CHAPTER FORTY-TWO

"Y OU'RE LOOKING FOR WILLIAM REINHARDT, AREN'T you?" Reena asked the redhead.

She nodded. "My name's Kandi. With an *i*. And a *K*."

"Of course it is." Reena smirked, her sarcasm floating well above Kandi's head.

She looked down at the small silk rose pinned to her dress. "They told me to wear this. Should I just wait here?"

Reena lowered her eyes to the flower. "The rose . . . ?"

"So he can find me?" Kandi explained, like Reena wasn't very bright.

Reena nodded her understanding, grateful for the little bit of good luck. "Actually, I was sent over by Mr. Reinhardt. Something has come up. I'm afraid he won't be requiring your services this evening."

"But I was booked for the whole night," she pouted.

Reena began propelling her toward the door, maneuvering to pluck the rose from her dress. "And I'm sure he will make good on the, er, invoice. Have a good evening, Kandi with a K."

"And an *i*."

Reena tried not to roll her eyes. "How could I forget?"

She watched Kandi walk away, and waited until the other woman was out of sight to pin the rose on her own dress.

A moment later, Reinhardt entered the room. The waiters and waitresses hurried to his side, eager to offer him hors d'oeuvres and champagne. Reena watched him preen, obviously enjoying the attention.

He made the rounds, meeting and greeting everyone in attendance. Reena wondered if it was her imagination that the locals seemed uncomfortable, their smiles stiff, their handshakes a little too effusive.

His gaze was pulled to hers, as if he could feel the weight of her stare. They locked eyes, Reena making a point to hold it just a little longer than necessary. His gaze slid to the rose pin at her breast.

A look of surprise passed briefly over his face. She gave him a slow, seductive smile.

Game on.

CHAPTER FORTY-THREE

"I'M NOT DOING THIS," CHARLIE SAID, HIS HAND ON the curve of Ava's lower back.

"We're just dancing, Charlie. We've done it before. Of course, that was when I thought it actually meant something. But still."

"Not here, not now," Charlie said between clenched teeth.

Ava pulled him in closer as the woman named Bo watched warily from the edge of the room. "I think a dance is the least that you owe me."

She looked over his shoulder, watching as Reinhardt moved toward Reena like a heat-seeking missile. He leaned in, whispering something in her ear. Reena nodded, and he put a hand on her back, guiding her to the door.

Ava hoped Reena would be okay. Somehow they had become more than comrades in arms. They had become friends. Ava wouldn't want anything to happen to her.

She refocused on Charlie, pressing seductively against him. Now that Reinhardt was gone, Charlie was all hers.

One song ended and a new one began, this one softer and slower. Charlie looked down at her, his gaze softening. Her resolve, moments before rock-solid, faltered under the heat of his deep blue stare. They had always had passion. Always had that mysterious brand of chemistry that was impossible to deny and just as impossible to force.

You either had it with someone, or you didn't.

She and Charlie had it in spades, and she was annoyed to find that it was still there, even after everything he'd done to her.

"We were good, weren't we?" Charlie remembered. "Before everything went bad?"

The reminder was just what she needed. Everything *had* gone bad. Worse than bad.

"Just answer me this, Charlie: Was any of it real?"

He stepped away, putting a few inches between their bodies, and twirled her. She fanned out, eyes still on his, before spinning back into him.

"Well?" she pressed, surprised to find she wanted an answer.

"It all got blurred together," he admitted.

"There's nothing you can say for certain wasn't a part of the con?"

He turned her around as the music changed again. They began to waltz slowly.

"Love," he said simply.

At first, Ava was thrown. It wasn't the answer she had expected. But then she realized Charlie's gaze was fixed not on her face, but on something just over her shoulder.

Glancing behind her, she saw the tall blonde approaching. He hadn't been speaking to her at all.

Had he?

Ava's and Charlie's bodies quickly unfurled.

"Love, this is—" Charlie began.

Bo extended an elegant hand. "Ava Winters, yes?"

They shook hands, Bo sizing up Ava with a narrowing of her made-up eyes.

"Charlie," Bo said, "there are some people I'd like you to meet." She looked at Ava. "Do you mind if I steal him for a minute?"

Ava shook her head. "Not at all."

Charlie leaned toward Ava as Bo turned away, heading for the bar. "Why are you here?"

"I just want to talk, Charlie."

"Here?"

"No, not here."

"Then where?"

Her stare was meaningful. "You know where."

CHAPTER FORTY-FOUR

IN AN ALCOVE OFF THE TASTING ROOM, REENA HAD
her hands full.

She'd been dodging Reinhardt's advances—left, right, and
literally in between—since they'd left the party. She'd had
enough batting of eyes and licking of lips to last a lifetime. It
disgusted her. He disgusted her. But it was important she play
the part of the debauched whore.

And play it she would.

For Cruz and everyone else Reinhardt had screwed over.

Reinhardt gawked at her like a starving hyena, running a
hand along her shoulder, dangerously close to her breast.

"I have a meeting upstairs in a half an hour," he said.
"Why don't you wait for me down here."

She moved closer, running a hand up his chest and biting her
lower lip. "A half an hour is a long time," she purred. "Maybe I
could keep you company until then."

She was going to listen in on that meeting, one way or
another.

"What do you have in mind?"

She leaned in, nibbling his ear. "Exactly what you paid for," she whispered.

He took her hand, pressing dry lips to her knuckles, his tongue flicking over her skin like slime. "I'll lead the way."

Reena followed him up the stairs, both exhilarated and scared. She didn't have the key to ruining him completely. Not yet. But they were close. She would play her part. She just hoped she could hold him off until Wells made his appearance.

Reinhardt wrapped his arm around her as they reached the top of the stairs, an elaborate chandelier hanging above them. For a moment, she imagined pushing his body over the railing, watching him slam into the marble below.

It would be so easy. And feel so good.

But that wouldn't save Simon. And it wasn't part of the mission.

His hand slid lower, squeezing her ass as they headed for the double doors at the end of the hall. She bit her inner cheek to hold back her repulsion, forcing a smile. She said she'd do anything for vengeance.

But as they entered Reinhardt's master suite, she just hoped she wouldn't have to.

CHAPTER FORTY-FIVE

"WE SHOULD BE IN THERE WITH THEM," JANE SAID, nervously tapping one heeled foot.

"Relax," Shay said. "We're staying here. If they need us, I'll take care of it."

They sat in Marie's sedan, watching a battalion of shaggy-haired valets in red suits park both vintage automobiles and electric cars as Reinhardt's security muscled around the front of the property.

Shay's cavalier attitude only served to make her angry. Everyone else was inside working while she stayed in the car with Shay like a little kid, too young to see the late show.

"Why did Takeda send me a dress if I'm going to be stuck in this car?" she asked.

"Everyone at the party is dressed up. We might be outside, but we still need to blend in," he explained.

"Why even bring me if I'm not going to do anything?" she fumed.

"So I can keep an eye on you."

She crossed her hands over her chest, knowing it made her look childish, but not caring.

"This is bullshit," she said. "Whatever—and whoever—is inside that estate might be able to unlock my memory. The only thing I have now is Takeda's training. I'm sick of everyone else making these decisions for me."

"Bullshit?" He grinned. "Well, I'm glad you have your voice back."

She turned to the window. "That doesn't let you off the hook."

Silence enveloped the car.

"I remember when I first saw you," he finally said, "lying on the bed in your *washitsu*. Takeda knew you'd come out of it stronger than ever, but me . . . I wasn't so sure."

She looked at him in surprise. "I don't remember seeing you on Rebun."

"Takeda assigned me to infiltrate Cain's organization. I left before you woke up."

"So Cain, Reinhardt . . . all of this, it's about you, too? Part of your revenge?" she asked, momentarily distracted from her anger by the possibility of learning something about Shay.

He looked away. "The difference between you and me, Jane, is that you have secrets you want to remember. I have secrets I wish I could forget."

"That's not an answer." She said it softly, not wanting to take advantage of Shay's unusual display of vulnerability. "But I have to admit that there has always been something familiar about you. Weird, since you left Rebun Island before I even woke up."

He put his hand gently on hers. "Does this help?"

She looked down at their hands, resting on the console of the sedan. Strangely, there was something familiar about it.

"Close your eyes," he said, his voice hoarse.

She did it without question.

"For the first two weeks you were on Rebun Island"—his voice wrapped around her like velvet in the hushed and darkened car—"I held your hand every night before bed. I even talked to you sometimes, although I didn't know if you could hear me. I told Takeda it was because I didn't want you to feel alone, but the truth is, I was more alone than anyone."

She opened her eyes, closing her hand around his, studying his scarred knuckles. "Now I know why you feel so familiar."

CHAPTER FORTY-SIX

REINHARDT KISSED REENA'S NECK AS HIS HAND
crept up Reena's thigh. They were in the large master
bedroom lying on his massive four-poster bed.

She slapped his hand away, trying to maintain a teasing
smile. She needed to string him along a little, keep him going
until the meeting with Wells.

Reinhardt chuckled.

"Maybe a drink," she suggested, "to loosen things up."

Ignoring the suggestion, he started sliding the dress off
her shoulder. "How about I quench your thirst instead?"

He touched his lips to her neck, traveling toward her chest.
She cringed, forcing herself not to pull away. She thought of
Cruz instead, his tender touch, the adoration in his eyes when
he looked at her.

But when Reinhardt's tongue moved farther downward,
she knew it was time for Plan B.

Reaching for her garter, she touched the small knife she'd
taken from Tavern Red, her own secret backup in case things
went wrong. She was holding the blade over his back, about to
carve the life out of him, when a knock sounded at the door.

He groaned, glancing at his fancy watch. Reena slid the knife back into her garter as he moved off the bed.

"Don't move," he said, heading for the door.

He opened the door, his voice a murmur as he greeted whomever was on the other side. A moment later, Senator Jacob Wells strode into the room.

Rage shrieked through Reena's brain at the sight of him, the man who had paid for the murder of her mother.

But it wasn't just rage. It was pain, too. The same crushing pain that had made Reena wonder if she would survive it in the months after her mother's death. She'd thought it was long dead, replaced by the vengeance she'd learned on Rebun Island. But seeing Jacob Wells brought it all back: the tumultuous relationship with her mother that was supposed to last a lifetime, the loss of the one person who had always been there for her, the person who had taught Reena how to be a fighter, a survivor. In the aftermath of her mother's murder, she'd come to realize that they only fought like they did because they were so alike.

She returned her attention to the knife, reaching for it again, as Wells moved into the room. Gripping the weapon, she considered her options. To kill Reinhardt and Wells now would satisfy her primal urge to see them pay, but it wouldn't free Simon. And Reena in prison wasn't what her mother would have wanted.

Instead, Reena pricked her thigh lightly with its blade, the self-inflicted pain snapping her out of the sea of emotion brought on by the appearance of Wells.

She needed to focus. She wasn't Reena Fuller anymore. Not tonight. She was Kandi with a K and an i.

Noticing Reena on the bed, Wells looked her up and down. "Who's this, William?"

Reinhardt winked. "Kandi here was just keeping me company while I waited for Cain. I haven't heard back from him since yesterday. Don't know where he could be."

Wells's gaze settled on Reena. She tried to stay calm, reminding herself that she didn't look anything like Senator Fuller's spoiled daughter.

Not tonight. Not anymore.

"I don't think we should be discussing business in front of your friend here," Wells finally said.

Reinhardt tipped his head to the adjoining bathroom. "Freshen up in the powder room. And don't come out until I call you."

Playing the part of the obedient floozy, Reena crossed the gleaming wood floors to the bathroom. Now that she was so close, she expected to be afraid. Instead, she was more resolved than ever. Reinhardt and Wells were pigs. She was going to cut deeply into their lives and make them bleed.

And if she had to die in the process, so be it.

She entered the bathroom, closing the door all the way for show. She waited a couple of minutes before easing it open just a crack.

"I haven't heard from him, either," Wells was saying. "Maybe he's changed his mind. Or worse, his tune."

"You're being paranoid," Reinhardt said, pouring himself a drink.

"There's a difference between paranoia and caution," Wells argued. "And being cautious, covering our tracks, is why we've been so successful."

CHAPTER FORTY-SEVEN

"I REMEMBER WHEN YOU DECIDED TO REFURBISH this room," Charlie said, looking around the renovated wine cellar. "You were so excited."

Ava followed his gaze, her sadness reborn. She never got the chance to finish it.

"It made me feel better to be down here," she said. "You made me feel better, too, back before I realized it was all an act."

He moved closer to her. "It wasn't all an act, Ava. I cared about you. I still do."

"Don't bother," she said. "Just tell me why? Why did you do it?"

He shrugged. "It was a business proposition. One I couldn't pass up."

Ava stroked the dark wood paneling. She'd spent hours picking it out, and now it did nothing but collect dust beneath her fallen kingdom.

"So you got control of the estate and Reinhardt paid you handsomely," she said. "Win-win."

"It wasn't a win-win. Because you lost. I see that now."
His voice was sincere.

Then again, it always had been.

She pinned him with her eyes. "Save it, Charlie. You didn't just steal my estate. You put it in the hands of the one man my family wanted to keep it from."

She moved in on him, grabbing the lapels of his suit and shoving him forcefully against the wall. It felt good to use Takeda's training in such a physical way. To use her new-found strength to subdue the man who had traded her love for money. She could hold her own now with almost anyone—and certainly with someone like Charlie.

And yet, standing so close, her body pressed against his, the smell of wine on his breath, she wanted not only to rip out his heart but in a strange and terrible way to rip off his clothes.

She shook her head. Why did he have to do this to her?

"Jesus, Charlie," she finally managed to say. "We weren't even married. How could you deceive me like that?"

But she was as mad at herself as she was at him. Maybe if she'd looked harder she would have seen Reinhardt's strings on his shoulders.

"You have to know that his plan to take Starling was in effect long before I came into the fold," he said.

"And that makes it okay? Everything you did to me?"

He shook his head. "You don't get it, do you? Reinhardt was going to get Starling one way or another. Sylvie could never be convinced. Could never be taken, either. He knew that. But without her in the picture, Reinhardt saw a rich target in your hopelessly romantic heart."

Dread dropped like a stone in her stomach. "What are you saying?"

"I'm saying, Ava, that the only way to get Starling was to remove your grandmother from the equation."

Ava stepped back, letting go of him. She shook her head. "My grandmother died of a heart attack."

Charlie shook his head. "You, more than anyone, should know that things aren't always as they seem."

CHAPTER FORTY-EIGHT

AVA DIDN'T KNOW HOW LONG THEY STOOD THERE, Charlie's revelation ringing through her ears like a bad song.

She was torn between wanting to guzzle the wine around her and wanting to smash the bottles wildly, destroying what was left of the grapes harvested under her family's careful watch.

As if that could somehow erase everything that had happened. As if by getting rid of the wine, she might be another Ava. An Ava who didn't own something worth so much that someone would kill for it.

She caressed a bottle of vintage red, the glass smooth and cool to the touch. Older wines were an intriguing beast. More delicious and vibrant than the younger breeds, old wine had a vastly shortened life span once opened. Like a dark secret, an old wine had to be handled with care. Otherwise, it would leave a terrible taste in the mouth of whomever consumed it.

Now it was time to serve Charlie his drink.

"You stole my world, Charlie Bay. It's only fair that you should lose yours."

"You can't do anything to me," Charlie scoffed. "I could have you removed from the premises with a flick of my wrist."

"The thing is," Ava continued as if he hadn't spoken, "you've had every opportunity to come clean, but we both know that's something you'll never do. You don't want to lose that Rolex on your wrist, the Benz in your driveway."

He considered her words, her calm demeanor causing a spark of fear to light his eyes. "I'll write you a check," he said. His tone was conciliatory. "It's only fair."

She ambled slowly around the cellar, gazing at the different wines. "You don't want redemption. You just want to put your sins to bed so you can sleep, too." She came to a stop in front of the portrait. "Tell me why you saved it."

"Why do you think?" he said, desperation creeping into his voice. "Ava, I still—"

"Don't." She stopped him. "Just tell me what they did to my grandmother. Tell me or I swear I'll—"

"You'll what?" Charlie said with a fresh show of fight. "You have no leverage over me. I mean, bloody hell, I'd tell you to go home but you don't even have that anymore. Just leave, Ava."

She moved toward her clutch, still on the shelf where she'd put it when she came down to meet Charlie. She turned to face him.

"Say good-bye to your world, Charlie. But not Napa Valley. This isn't your real life. Your real life was a blue-collar family in London, your father a history teacher with all of your good looks and none of your tact, your mother a florist who wishes you would call more."

Charlie was visibly thrown. Ava had expected it. He'd told her his parents had died when he was young.

She handed him the manila envelope.

"What is this?" Charlie said, trepidation in his voice.

Ava continued as if he hadn't spoken. "Your dad's quite the ladies' man, isn't he? Like you. Only it seems he likes them a tad younger." She watched as he stared at the pictures inside the envelope. "Don't bother tearing them up. I've got copies."

He looked up at her with horror in his eyes. "Where did you get these?"

"That doesn't really matter, now does it? You took all that I had left of my family, Charlie. Why shouldn't I do the same to you?"

He shook his head. "You don't understand . . . My mother's a good person. This will destroy her."

"You knew all along," Ava said. "You knew what your father was doing and never said a word."

"I discovered the truth when I was eighteen," he explained. "I begged my father to stop. And when the police got involved—"

"Your dad paid them to keep the records sealed." Ava handed Charlie wire receipts from his father's checking to a dummy account set up by the three officers who originally arrested him. "Another piece of information I assume you don't want going public."

Charlie grabbed on to one of the wine racks to steady himself. "What are you going to do with all of this?"

Ava shrugged. "I'm more interested in how your mother is going to react when she learns she's been married to a pedophile for the past thirty-one years. And just imagine what the head of the school district will say—"

"You can't," Charlie protested. "My mother . . . She won't

be able to handle it. And my father . . . He's sick, Ava. He needs help."

"You should have done something about that before, Charlie. Or should I say Edward? Edward Charles Bayley."

"Please don't do this," he pleaded .

"Tell me what Reinhardt did to my grandmother and maybe I'll consider it."

Charlie spoke fast. "All I know is that someone told Reinhardt there was no way Sylvie would sell, especially not to him. Whoever it was said that you could be manipulated, but only if Sylvie was out of the picture."

Ava's mind reeled as she processed the implications. "Who are you talking about?"

"Reinhardt never told me who it was, but I assumed it was someone who knew your family—and Sylvie—well. Someone who could get close enough to Sylvie to take her out."

She looked at him in horror. "Marie?"

CHAPTER FORTY-NINE

R EENA LISTENED CAREFULLY THROUGH THE CRACK in the door.

"I can't just sit around waiting for him," Wells said. "Just being here makes me susceptible to public scrutiny."

Reinhardt set down his glass. "Fine. Tell me where Marcus is and I'll relay the information."

"I don't know . . ."

Reena saw Wells walk to the window, but she didn't know what he was doing until Reinhardt spoke a second later.

"I've already tried calling him," Reinhardt protested. "If he doesn't answer this time, you give me the information, and we go forward with our plans."

An electronic beep sounded through the room as Wells disconnected the call. He sighed. "Darren Marcus is living in Sacramento, in an apartment above a Thai restaurant called Lu's Palace. Tell Cain to make it look like a suicide."

"The guy's totally under the radar, Jacob. We don't need to be that careful," Reinhardt insisted.

It was a reckless assertion, in stark contrast to Wells's

paranoia. Reena tattooed the information on her memory like the circle on her neck.

"Actually, I'd rather not know how he's taken care of," Wells decided. "I'm just glad she found him. Once again, she's proven herself useful. Last time, we wrote her a check. I think it's only fitting we do the same this time around, don't you?"

Reena watched as Reinhardt walked over to the oak dresser. He pulled open the top drawer, removing a checkbook.

"I hadn't even realized you asked her to find him," Reinhardt said as he wrote.

Wells shook his head. "I didn't. She approached me. Wanted to know what else she could do to make sure Ava Winters never redeems the keys to her castle."

Reena stepped back from the door, leaning against the cold tiles of the bathroom wall. Someone had it out for Ava. Someone was feeding Reinhardt and Wells information to keep Ava from reclaiming Starling.

She filed the information away and moved back to the door, scanning the room until she found Reinhardt. He was standing near the dresser, holding a small silver picture frame. Reena couldn't see the photograph inside it, but it seemed to hold Reinhardt captive.

"Put that away," Wells said with a hint of exasperation. "You did what had to be done. We all did. Self-preservation is worth a thousand lives."

"I didn't care about a thousand lives," Reinhardt growled. "I only cared about one."

Reena jockeyed for a better view, trying to figure out who was in Reinhardt's picture frame. Anyone Reinhardt cared about was a potential weakness, something to be exploited in their quest for revenge.

"Yes, well, you only go around once. Damn the people who get in your way. Isn't that what you used to say?" Wells asked his former college roommate. "And we've done better than most. We have everything we ever wanted."

"Do we, Jacob?" Reinhardt asked, his temper exploding. "Do we have everything we ever wanted? And if so, at what cost?" He continued without waiting for Wells to answer. "No, don't answer. I'll tell you. The only thing my money can't buy. My little girl."

Reinhardt threw the photograph maniacally against the wall, the glass frame shattering on impact. It skidded across the wood floor, coming to rest near the bathroom door.

Reena moved around, adjusting her vantage point through the narrow opening, hoping for a clear look at the picture lying on the floor, covered in shards of broken glass.

And then she saw it: a picture of William Reinhardt with a young woman. Reinhardt had his arm wrapped around the woman, the smile on his face making him almost unrecognizable as the monster who had slobbered all over her in the bedroom.

But it wasn't William's face that drew Reena's gaze. It was the engaging, bright-eyed beauty beside him, her long blond hair falling in a glossy sheet around delicate features that Reena would recognize anywhere.

The young woman next to William Reinhardt was Jane.

CHAPTER FIFTY

J ANE EASED OUT OF THE CAR, OFFERING A SILENT apology to Shay, slumped over in the seat with an already-swelling welt on his head. She hadn't wanted to knock him unconscious, but it was the only way she was going to get the answers she needed.

She hurried down the road, watching as groups of people exited the estate and a few late arrivals made their way to the main house. The valets hustled back and forth, bringing some cars and parking others, as guests stood around in dresses and tuxedos.

Jane stepped onto the grounds and walked toward the front door.

CHAPTER FIFTY-ONE

"MY FAMILY ISN'T RESPONSIBLE FOR THE THINGS I've done," Charlie said. "You don't have to do this to them."

Still reeling from the suspicion that Marie had been helping Reinhardt, Ava's resolve began to soften under Charlie's pleading. Ava wasn't a bad person. In fact, she had always gone out of her way to help other people. Maybe Charlie was right.

Maybe this was revenge taken too far. After all, she'd made her point.

Charlie moved closer, reaching up to touch her face. "I'm so sorry, Ava. I . . ." He shook his head. "I wish I could take it all back."

The moment their bodies were in orbit, the pull was too great to fight. All at once, Ava wasn't remembering the pain and heartache of the weeks following Charlie's betrayal, the stinging shame of her naïveté. She was transported instead to the picnics she and Charlie had, hours spent talking and laughing under the warm Napa sun. She remembered lying in bed, planning their future, naming their children, feeling that nothing in the world could ever hurt her as long as Charlie was by her side.

He ran his hand through her hair, her head tipping involuntarily into his palm. She closed her eyes, desperately clinging to the possibility that he had changed. He had saved the painting. Maybe he was trying to save his soul, too.

"Ava . . . ," he murmured.

And then, her greatest betrayal as Charlie lowered his lips to hers, capturing her mouth, desire licking like fire through her body. For a moment there was nothing else. No lies. No past. No hurt. Just his tongue exploring her mouth, his body pressed against hers like a treasured memory.

And then, from the clutch in her hand, something jabbed her palm. She hesitated, breaking their kiss.

"What is it?" Charlie asked, his breath coming fast and heavy.

Opening the clutch, she found the jagged piece of Acala's flame. She remembered Takeda's words. *Burning away all weaknesses is the only way to find enlightenment.*

To become the warrior she needed to be. To truly enact *fukushuu* against this man who took her home. Her family. Her life. And yes, her heart.

Charlie waits anxiously under an impressive arch adorned with white calla lilies, watching Ava saunter down the aisle in an elegant Vera Wang peau de soie gown. It's a small gathering—tasteful and intimate, exactly what Ava wants. Pachelbel's Canon in D resounds from the tiny iPod speakers Daniella has set up between masses of white hydrangeas.

Ava's sparkling sapphire necklace glitters in the sunlight—

her something blue. The aging grapes of Starling Vineyards create a stunning backdrop—her something old. Ava is blissful. It's a perfect day to get married and she's marrying the perfect guy.

Next to Charlie stands the man he has paid to pose as Rev. Moore. Charlie's smile is genuine. His feelings are real, but so is his deal with Reinhardt. And sadly, that deal has more power than his feelings will ever possess. That deal has already sealed his and Ava's fate.

Ava reaches Charlie and touches his face. "You are my something new." Charlie is aware of the irony in the fact that her words calm him. Part of Charlie would love to be her something old one day, too. However, the ominous-looking limousine waiting in the distance reminds him that his future is no longer up to him.

With Marie, Daniella, and a few select friends watching, Ava and Charlie are wed, or at least that's how it appears. The guests applaud as the bride and groom share that all-important kiss. Ava pulls back, a look of concern crossing her face.

"What is it, love?" Charlie asks cautiously.

"I forgot my something borrowed."

Charlie breathes a silent sigh of relief and reaches into his pocket. "Here, take this," he says as he offers her the Starling Vineyards cork souvenir key chain she gave him the first time they met. They kiss again, this time with even more passion.

As the couple walks back up the aisle, they greet their guests. "It's like a fairy tale, Ava," Daniella tells her as the old friends take a moment alone.

Charlie works his way toward the limousine. A window rolls down revealing William Reinhardt languishing in

the rich leather upholstery. "Bravo, young man. Helluva per-
formance."

"She's a good person," Charlie adds, almost a plea.

Reinhardt reminds Charlie that there was another option,
the one where the wedding would be real and a terrible acci-
dent would befall the young bride, leaving her husband to
inherit the entire estate and sell it to Reinhardt for pennies
on the dollar. Charlie cringes at the thought, a crashing real-
ization of how he ended up here in the first place.

Reinhardt smiles smugly at Charlie's visceral reaction. "That's
why we've gone with Plan B. The one where no one dies. Either
way, I'm soon to be Starling's one and only owner."

There's no easy way out for Charlie. Or for Ava. So in the
end, he's going to choose himself. But at least this path keeps
Ava alive.

Charlie gave it only a passing glance before bending his
head and trailing kisses along the side of her neck, picking up
where they left off.

Ava pushed him away. "No."

He looked up, his eyes clouded with desire. "We can make
it work, Ava. Start over."

"We're done, Charlie. We're done, and you're done."

She reached for the manila envelope, removing the final
piece of paper and shoving it into Charlie's chest.

He looked at it. "My God, Ava . . . You've already alerted
the authorities?"

The article was from the London *Times* and chronicled the
investigation into Clive Bayley for "inappropriate contact"
with students at the school where he taught history. Bayley

was currently on a leave of absence from the school and would likely be convicted and imprisoned. Penelope Bayley, Charlie's mother, was holed up in her home, avoiding the press and trying to come to terms with the realization that the man she called her husband was a stranger to her.

Ironically, it was something Ava could relate to wholeheartedly.

Charlie stumbled backward, collapsing against the wall of the cellar. "I can't believe you would do this. It's . . . it's despicable."

"No, Charlie. It's payback." She dropped the piece of Acala's flame at his feet. "Here. I don't need this anymore."

Stepping past him, she took one last look at the painting. She didn't think it was her imagination that the eyes of Sylvie and her mother were proud. She may not have gotten Starling back yet, but it was a start.

She glided toward the door leading to the vineyard. She had one foot on the stairs when Charlie's voice, weak and small, found her.

"My mother . . . Ava, you don't understand. She doesn't deserve this. She's a good person. A *good* person."

"So was I."

Daylight breaks on Rebun Island as Ava readies herself for a swim. Draped in a small karate gi, Ava touches the arch of her right foot against the salty foam.

It's chillier than she expected.

No one knows that better than Emily, who steps out of the water, fresh from her own swim. "You get used to it," she says, walking out of the water.

Ava can tell she's at home in the sea.

"Did Takeda suggest you take a swim?" Emily asks, her blond hair shining as the sun melts into the horizon. Her warmth is usually reserved for people she cares about or people she respects. Anyone training under Takeda, Emily figures, must be worthy of the latter, at least.

"I just need an outlet, I guess," Ava explains.

But as her ankles submerge into the icy trenches, she's not sure it's such a good idea.

"It's a quandary, isn't it?" Emily states, watching Ava's struggle. "If you jump right in, you'll freeze, jolting your body into a state of shock. But if you enter too slowly . . ."

"I'll psych myself out. I may never go in."

Emily nods, appreciates Ava's understanding.

"I'm just . . . I get so angry sometimes, you know?" Ava asks.

Emily rubs her bare soles in the sand. "You have to focus that energy, not let it deter you. Think of it not as an emotion, but as a distraction. Especially if you want revenge."

Ava closes her eyes. That's exactly what she wants. Without so much as a warning, Ava lets her body fall into the water. A few shallow-dwelling fish scurry away, startled by her presence.

As Ava wades, she feels a sudden need to confess, "This isn't me, you know."

Emily almost lets out a laugh. There's no sense explaining or justifying her presence to fellow trainees. This may be the only place in the world where her plight is truly understood, respected, and supported. Emily knows what Ava is feeling because Emily feels it, too.

"Sometimes I question myself, my motives . . . ," Ava says

as her fingers begin to prune. "I mean, I'm here to learn how to destroy people. I used to be a good person."

Emily darkens at this comment, remembering her own past, before her father was taken from her. Rolling around with her dog Sammy and best friend Jack in sand that felt much like the kind she's standing on now. But the two landscapes are a world apart. Much like Emily has grown decidedly distant from the little girl who once collected sea glass on the beach. She can still hear Amanda Clarke's pure, wholesome giggle ringing in her head.

"It's just . . . ," Ava starts. She shrugs, repeating the words again. "I used to be a good person."

Emily looks at her, considers the comment, those weighty, steely eyes perfectly composed. She thinks back on her father holding her hand as they walked along the beach. She wishes that she could tell the little girl that the moment is fleeting, that she should hold on to it as long as she can. That she should hold on to her father's hand as long as she can.

Emily closes her eyes. "So was I."

CHAPTER FIFTY-TWO

REENA WALKED OVER TO THE MIRROR IN THE POW-
der room, still shocked at the revelations from William
Reinhardt's meeting with Jacob Wells. Looking at her reflection, she barely recognized herself.

Everything had become very grave, the stakes so high in a
life that used to be a roll of the dice. Dance clubs and camera
mobs had given way to a singular mission. It wasn't the life
Reena's mother would have wanted for her only child.

Then again, if Reena was just like her, as Gloria always
claimed, then perhaps she would understand.

*A nine-year-old Reena, tightly wrapped under her comforter,
lies securely in bed as her mother combs through the bookcase
in Reena's room for the perfect bedtime story.*

*"I'd rather you tell me about this, Mommy," Reena says,
motioning to the dream catcher dangling above her head.
The circle covered with netting catches more than just dreams.
It has Reena's attention, something that isn't easy to do.*

Gloria explains that it was a gift Reena's father gave her on their wedding day, a promise to always keep the way they're feeling right now in their dreams. In their hearts.

"But he left us," Reena says, confused and saddened at the rare mention of him.

"Just because we're hurting doesn't mean we should forget the good." A young Reena tries to accept this. Her mother unhooks the dream catcher and hands it to Reena. "Why don't you hold it for tonight?"

"Do you have dreams, Mommy?"

Gloria smiles to herself. "Well, I once thought about being a congressman or maybe even a senator. Of making a difference."

Reena suddenly reaches into the dream catcher, ripping out the netting.

Startled, Gloria takes it back from her. "Honey, why did you do that?"

Reena smiles. "How can your dreams make it out into the world if they're stuck in the net?"

Gloria loves her daughter's way of thinking. She places the dream catcher back up on the hook. It's just a circle now. But with greater meaning.

"From now on, all your dreams, everything you want in life, will go through this circle and out into the world. It's not a dream catcher," her mother says. "It's a dream portal."

Gloria kisses her daughter's forehead. "What do you want to go through the portal?" she asks her daughter. "Be careful, because whatever you put in there, whatever you want, just might come true."

Reena smiles. "I just want you to love me forever."

> *Gloria jokingly pretends to think about it for an exagger-*
> *ated moment or two, then leans close, whispering in her daugh-*
> *ter's ear.*
> *"Done."*

The memory lingered as Reena studied herself in the mirror. Finally, she brought her hands to her face and methodically removed the prosthetic nose, peeling it off slowly so that it didn't tear her skin. She would be recognized this way.

And that was the plan.

She took a deep breath and turned toward the bathroom door, flinging it open.

"What the hell do you think you're doing?" Reinhardt shouted. "Get back in there until I tell you to come out."

"I thought I heard you call my name," she said, not bothering to be polite. "Sorry."

She turned away, pivoting in front of Wells until he had a perfect view of her back. She pulled her platinum wig into a bun the way her mother had her wear it at political events, knowing it would reveal the circle tattoo—the dream catcher without a net—on her neck.

"Stop right there!" Wells shouted, storming toward her.

He spun her around, tearing off the wig and grabbing her head, staring at her face with piercing eyes. Then he turned her around, tracing the shape of the tattoo with his finger.

CHAPTER FIFTY-THREE

"Watch where you're going," Jacob Wells murmurs as Reena knocks into him backstage at a press conference. The file he's holding falls to the ground, index cards and papers scattering like leaves.

"Last I checked, you're not my boss," Reena shoots back, as defiant as ever. She's in her prime, basking in the light that shines down on her mother.

"I will be soon," he mutters.

This gets Reena's attention. She loves a good sparring match. "You really think you're going to win?"

But Wells is confident the election is his, almost as if he knows something she doesn't.

Reena looks down, noticing the papers. Figuring she'll be the bigger person, she goes to pick them up. When she rises to stand, she notices Wells staring at her.

"It's a dream catcher," she says. And then, "You wouldn't understand."

He holds out a hand for his papers, but when she goes to give them to him, she pulls them back, just to mess with him. She's being a brat, but Wells has it coming.

She glances down at the papers, unsettled by what she sees. "What is this?"

Wells grabs it from her, walking away in a huff.

Just then, Cruz Benton comes over, sidling up next to Reena.

"What a creep," he says.

"And you're not?"

Cruz smiles. He likes her style. "Name's Cruz Benton. I work—"

"For my mother. I know."

"So then you're saying I shouldn't have spent the last forty minutes getting up the courage to introduce myself?"

Reena can't help but laugh. Then she grows serious.

"He had some papers in his hand. They were kind of weird."

"If by 'weird' you mean 'boring,' you're absolutely right," Cruz says. "We have mountains of boring information. Facts, figures, statistics . . ."

Reena shakes her head. "It was a list. Of everyone who's a part of Mom's staff. Mindy. Joseph. Linda. Eric. Their spouses, their kids. My name. Your name. And who's Simon?"

Cruz went still. "He was on there, too?"

Reena just nods.

"MEET REENA FULLER," WELLS SAID, TURNING HER face toward Reinhardt.

"Gloria Fuller's daughter?" Reinhardt asked, shock and disbelief warring on his face.

"The very same," Wells confirmed.

Reena stood her ground, oddly numb. There was a distant

part of her that was genuinely frightened, but her fear couldn't seem to break free of the adrenaline coursing through her veins.

"What are you doing here?" Reinhardt demanded.

Reena didn't answer.

"I knew it," Wells muttered, shaking his head. "We should have found her and taken care of her at the start of all this. Loose ends always come back to bite us in the ass."

"Last chance," Reinhardt said, pulling her hair to tip her head back. "Why are you here?"

He shoved her at Wells and stalked across the room, opening the nightstand by his bed. When he turned around, he was holding an ominous-looking handgun.

"If we can't make you talk, maybe this will."

Reena was silent. It was all part of the plan. She just hoped they didn't pull the trigger before she saw it through.

CHAPTER FIFTY-FOUR

"SHAY! WAKE UP!" AVA SLAPPED SHAY'S CHEEKS, trying to bring him around.

She was kneeling in the passenger seat, wiping blood from his forehead with a rag from the glove compartment. He had a wicked-looking welt on his forehead and Jane was nowhere to be found. She was a fighter, but the idea of her in Reinhardt's hands still made Ava sick with worry.

"C'mon, Shay," Ava muttered. "Don't do this. Not now. Get up."

She looked frantically around the car, trying to find something that would wake him up, finally setting on a half-full water bottle in the passenger-side footwell.

She picked it up, uncapped it, and dumped the entire contents over Shay's head.

He came to swinging, and Ava leaned back, trying to avoid his significant fists.

"Whoa, whoa, whoa!" she said, leaning away. "It's me, Ava!"

"Ava?" He sat up and looked around, touching a hand to the welt on his forehead, then his hair, dripping onto his face. "What's going on?"

"I'm sorry. I had to wake you up." She looked into his eyes. "Where's Jane?"

"Who do you think did this to me?" he said, looking at his head in the rearview mirror.

"Wait a minute . . . Jane did this to you?"

He nodded. "Guess she got sick of my company."

Ava sighed. "Great. Now what?"

"I don't know about you," Shay said, "but I could use an aspirin. Or a drink. Or both."

"Well, I don't have either," Ava said.

"What good are you, then?" Shay stammered, tipping his head back and closing his eyes.

Ava slapped him. Hard. "Am I the only one who's worried here? Jane is gone." She said it slowly since he didn't seem to understand the magnitude of the situation. "And how did she manage to nail you anyway?"

"She distracted me," he said simply.

"She distracted you?" Ava repeated, trying to figure out how little Jane could distract Shay Thomas, veteran police officer and Takeda's own protégé.

Shay avoided her gaze, clearly too embarrassed by his lapse to say more about it.

"What do we do now?"

He opened the car door. "We go in there and find her before they do."

CHAPTER FIFTY-FIVE

A S SOON AS SHE ENTERED THE FOYER, JANE KNEW that she'd been in the house before.

She'd maneuvered her way past the guards without incident, just another pretty face in a party full of them, and headed straight for the stairs. Guided by some kind of strange intuition, she made her way to the second-floor hall, then stopped at the third doorway on the left. Placing her hand on the bronze knob, she pushed open the door and turned on the light.

Recognition slammed into her.

She crossed the room to the bed and dropped onto the pale pink comforter, surveying the room. It was elaborately appointed, the white walls offset by a rich mahogany bed, matching dresser, and vanity. A massive armoire sat to the right of a mirrored door that Jane somehow knew was to a large walk-in closet.

Standing, she turned her attention to the knickknacks and awards that decorated the dresser, her gaze coming to rest on an intricately detailed music box. She picked it up and opened the lid. A tinny refrain that she recognized as Chopin's Nocturne in C-sharp echoed through the room.

Jane looked inside the music box, her eyes drawn to a pair of ruby earrings. She lifted them to the light, recognizing them from a memory she'd had while at Marie's house.

Closing the music box, she leaned into the dresser, studying a porcelain doll encased in glass. It was obviously old, its cheeks tinged brown, its eyes eerie and glazed. Oddly, Jane could relate to its frozen glare.

She removed the glass enclosure and picked up the doll, rubbing the cool porcelain against her cheek. Her mind raced backward.

Seven-year-old Jane sits in the back of a limo, her legs dangling, unable to reach the luxury car's matted floor. A large man sits across from her, the smell of his aged Lagavulin single malt overwhelming, as an equally impressive man sits by the little girl's side: her father.

He puts his arm around Jane's shoulder, whispers in her ear. "Don't worry, sweetheart; Daddy's meeting is over. We'll get to spend the whole day together now. I just have one quick stop to make."

Jane looks up at him. She loves spending time with her father.

The limo pulls up to a bar built to look like an old Spanish mission. Its name—Tavern Red—is lit up in flickering neon light.

The big man across from her puts his glass down, shakes William Reinhardt's hand, and leaves the limo.

Now that they're alone, and Jane's been such a good girl, William hands her a gift box.

She takes it, asking what it's for.

"It's for you. Plain and simple. Don't need an occasion to give you a gift, do I?" His deep, aggressive voice makes most people nervous, but to Jane, it's as harmonious as the music box on her dresser.

Jane opens the gift, thrilled to see her very own china doll. Just what she's been wanting. Reinhardt lowers the limo's divider and commands the driver to head to Napa Valley. The driver asks where exactly in Napa they're going.

"Starling Vineyards. I've got a proposition for the owner. She's a tough one," he says, then looks at his daughter with a wink. "But Daddy'll crack her."

Jane is too busy playing with her new doll to care. She thanks him again.

Reinhardt smiles.

Emerging from the memory, Jane turned her attention to a stack of certificates and awards from school competitions and extracurricular activities. It appeared she had gone to boarding school, taken karate and tai kwon do, ridden horses competitively, and sailed extensively.

She leaned in, looking more closely at a certificate of completion from an aviation academy; a photograph tucked into the frame showed her standing next to a small propeller plane.

"Flying lessons," Jane murmured.

She looked at it all, finally understanding. She wasn't some kind of badass genius. Just a spoiled rich girl who'd had the luxury of learning and experiencing everything that interested her.

And then she saw something else. Something on the aviation certificate that had escaped her notice on everything else.

We are pleased to award this Certificate of Completion to Mira Reinhardt . . .

Mira Reinhardt.

Mira. Reinhardt.

She dropped the stack of certificates, horror washing over her. She was William Reinhardt's daughter.

Her father had helped kill Reena's mother, had destroyed Ava's life.

"Oh, God . . ." Jane stumbled backward, the wheels of her mind turning.

If he was capable of murder, or betrayal, or theft . . . was he also behind what happened to her?

Her attention was pulled away from the possibility by the sound of shouting outside her room. She went to the door and listened.

The voice was deep and aggressive. Intimidating.

And familiar.

Sixteen-year-old Mira Reinhardt is sitting shotgun in her boyfriend Tim's candy-apple-red Mustang as they pull into Starling Vineyards' large circular driveway. Tim's house is just ten minutes away on the other side of town, in an afflu- ent neighborhood that prides itself on old money. Still, it's nothing compared to Starling.

"This is it," Mira says, as Tim, draped in a popped collar and low-sitting baseball cap, hops out of the car to open the door for his new lady, proving that chivalry isn't dead. At

least not to a sixteen-year-old boy who's dating the hottest girl in his class—and wants to keep it that way.

"Starling," Tim says in awe of the landscape. Mira mentions it's some kind of bird or something, she's not really sure.

Tim and Mira pass the marble fountain. She runs her hand through the water and flicks some back Tim's way with a flirty giggle. Mira's truly happy, frighteningly unaware of the fate that lies ahead.

Tim looks around at the lavish estate, asking Mira what it must be like to live in a place as opulent as this. "I don't know yet, we just moved in," she says, grabbing his arm and moving her boyfriend along. "C'mon, let's go upstairs," she says suggestively.

They walk up the stairs, Tim noting the elegant beauty of the cathedral-like home Mira's father recently acquired. She's used to her dad's frequent acquisition of businesses and houses, but this place is different. It's so gorgeous and meticulously designed, as if the people who lived here had planned to stay forever. She wonders why they left. Where they've gone.

Tim takes in every last detail of Mira as she walks up the stairs. Mira notices his appreciation of her. They stop on the stairs and kiss the way only teenagers can. Tim pulls away, asking if her father's home. But Mira just shrugs—even if he is, he's too busy to care.

Mira takes Tim's hand as they continue toward her bedroom. Tim asks about a rectangle of faded paint on the wall. Seems something used to hang here. Mira mentions there was a painting when they first arrived, a gorgeous portrait of three women.

"Perhaps they were the original owners?" Tim reasons, but

Mira's already thinking about what can go in its place. Maybe she'll take an art class in the fall and replace it with something new and original. Tim wonders how she'll find the time, given her tennis, equestrian, and aviation lessons.

Mira wraps her arms around Tim. She finds time for this, doesn't she?

Mira stops inches from her father's master suite, hearing deep voices looming from within. Mira suggests that today's the day Tim finally meets her father. Tim doesn't like the sound of that, but Mira tells him to relax—it'll be fine. They approach the door, but before she opens it, she realizes her dad and two other men are speaking in the most serious of tones. Mira tells Tim to hang on for a moment, and listens.

"We shouldn't be doing this," Tim says, but Mira shushes him, eavesdropping diligently.

"So then it's settled. You'll take her out."

Mira's heart begins to pound. What are they talking about?

"I've got the right guy to do it," Cain says, "Darren Marcus."

Reinhardt wants to know if he's loyal. Cain snickers— they're all loyal, till they're not. "And if that happens, we'll deal with him accordingly. Just like we're dealing with this Senator Fuller situation." Wells explains this can never be traced back to him. The assassination, or this meeting. But that's not a problem. The problem is figuring out who's going to take the fall. Wells says that's already taken care of, as he presents a photograph of Simon and Cruz Benton. Cruz works for Senator Fuller, so they'll make it appear as if his brother Simon used Cruz's name to sneak in the back, past security at the upcoming state capitol event in Sacramento. They can't pin it on Cruz because he'll be working all that day and have alibis. But Simon is on vacation from college and isn't being watched.

"What's his motivation?"

"He killed his abusive father when he was eleven. The courts ruled it self-defense, but it's still on record. Last week we arranged for someone to start a bar fight with him up in Boston after he had a few drinks. Kid was arrested, though no charges were filed."

Mira and Tim don't know what to do with this knowledge. They are flustered, don't know where to turn. They bump into each other and Tim drops his keys, the sound seems to echo throughout the house. Reinhardt opens the door. Standing behind him are Wells and Cain. The three men look at Mira, her father particularly troubled by her possibly having overheard. "Mira, get out of here. Take this boy with you."

"Dad, I—"

"LEAVE. NOW." Mira doesn't need to be told again. As she goes, Cain and Wells trade looks. They wonder how much she and the boy heard. Reinhardt tells them not to worry— his daughter didn't hear anything.

But Wells and Cain aren't so sure. And don't want anyone getting in their way.

CHAPTER FIFTY-SIX

AVA AND SHAY ENTERED AVA'S SECRET ROOM, planning to make their way into the main house from the restored cellar.

They were at the top of the stairs inside the main pantry when she grabbed Shay's arms.

"What?" he hissed. "We need to find Jane."

"I know we need to find Jane, but why are you freaking out? Why is it so wrong for her to see Reinhardt if he's her father?"

Shay's eyes glinted in the semidarkness. "Because he's the one who tried to kill her. He thinks she's dead, Ava. And if he figures out she's not, he's going to change that."

THE BARREL OF THE GUN, COLD AND HARD, PRESSED against Reena's cheek.

"Still not talking?" Reinhardt asked.

She didn't say anything. She was playing a dangerous game, waiting until the last minute to play her final card.

There was always a risk she would miscalculate and wait too long, something of which she was acutely aware with the gun so close to her brain.

"Just pull the trigger," Wells said. "If someone was coming for her, she would have said something by now."

Reinhardt cocked the gun.

"Aren't you afraid you'll make a mess on your perfect white walls?" she said.

Reinhardt hesitated. "The peace of mind will be worth the extra effort."

There was a long moment in which Reena wondered if she'd waited too long, half-expecting to hear the roar of the gun rip through the room.

"Okay, okay, don't shoot!" she said, readying herself for the next phase of the plan.

Reinhardt and Wells exchanged satisfied glances.

"It was Charlie," she said. "Charlie's the one who hired me to spy on you."

Wells immediately went for Reinhardt's throat. "You said we could trust him!"

Reinhardt shook his head. "She's lying. Charlie's in as deep as we are. He has just as much to lose."

But Reena could hear the doubt creeping into his voice.

"If she's lying, how does she even know about him?" Wells demanded.

"Please," Reena begged, playing the part of the frightened captive. "Don't hurt me. Charlie put me up to it."

"Why would he do that?" Reinhardt asked, pressing the gun more firmly into her cheek.

"He wants to ruin you," she said. "He paid me to get into your little meeting and find out where Marcus is."

Reinhardt's face went still as he considered her words.

"This is just great," Wells said. "For all we know, your little con man got to Cain. Maybe that's why we haven't been able to get ahold of him."

It was working. Reena couldn't believe it. In just a few minutes, with just a few well-chosen words, Charlie was being stripped of the trust he'd worked for years to build with Reinhardt.

And now that he didn't have his old life to fall back on—thanks to Ava—Charlie had nothing.

Which meant at least one of their targets had been successfully shattered.

"We need to get rid of him," Wells asserted nervously. "He's working with Cain to destroy us."

Reinhardt shook his head. "We don't know that."

"Don't be stupid!" Wells shouted.

"Why would they do that?" Reinhardt asked. "We've given them everything they've wanted."

"Why does any man do anything, William? Not for love—that's for children. And not for money, because there's always a way to get that. But power . . . now that's something worth fighting for. Your sidekick wants to dethrone you, my friend. And he's planning to make me a casualty in his little coup." Wells shook his head. "He knows too much. We can't afford to take the chance."

"What about Fuller's daughter?" Reinhardt asked.

Wells walked over, removing the gun from Reinhardt's

hand. He pressed it against Reena's temple. "I think you know the answer to that question."

JUST OUTSIDE THE DOOR IN THE HALLWAY, JANE AP-proached her father's master suite, following the sound of his muffled voice. She didn't know if she was prepared to face him. He was just a man she didn't even remember outside of a handful of muddled memories and a white-faced toy.

But whoever she'd been before waking up on Rebun, she wasn't that person anymore. And how could she embrace the person she was, the person she'd *become*, without facing the person she'd been?

She grasped the doorknob, preparing to face her father.

CHAPTER FIFTY-SEVEN

"LOOK AT IT THIS WAY," WELLS SAID. "WE'RE DOING you a favor, reuniting you with your mother."

Remembering Takeda's words, Reena masked her rage, consigning emotion to a dark corner of her mind where it couldn't affect her mission.

"Do what you want," she said. "But if you kill me, then you better start running. Out of Napa, and into hiding."

"What are you talking about?" shouted Wells impatiently.

The gun was still pointed at her, but he wasn't shooting. Not now. He was too interested in what she had to say next.

Reena laughed. "You don't think Charlie knows I'm in here? He's been collecting information on you guys for months. And he has almost enough to bring you down. Killing me would be the last piece of the puzzle to send you away for a very long time."

Lowering the gun, Wells grabbed Reinhardt and pulled him aside. They spoke in low murmurs as Reena watched their frenzied discussion with satisfaction.

Finally, Reinhardt walked back over to her. "Let's make a deal, Miss Fuller."

"I'm listening," she said.

"We'll double whatever Charlie's paying you." His tone was almost conciliatory. "In return, you leave Napa and never come back, never speak a word of this to anyone."

"And if you do," Wells said, "they'll be the last words you ever speak."

"What about Charlie?" Reena asked, playing her part to the hilt. "He'll come after me if I betray him."

"We'll take care of Charlie," Wells said.

Reena pretended to think about it. "Deal. But I don't want your money."

Reinhardt narrowed his eyes. "What do you want?"

She gave them a slow smile. "Let's just say it's enough to know what I know. Call it my own little insurance policy."

"Just remember," Wells said, "that tattoo on your neck is more than a circle. It's a permanent target. If you ever talk, we'll come for you, just like we came for your mother."

Reena stepped closer to the man who had eradicated her family for a new suit and a used Senate seat. She whispered something in his ear and turned for the door.

JANE CLOSED HER EYES, BRACING HERSELF FOR THE impending confrontation. She had wanted the truth, only the truth, for so long. But now that it was in front of her, she felt nothing but fear.

She glanced around the magnificent house. A palace with a dark and dangerous underside. Even before she'd lost her memory, she'd been living in a palace of secrets and lies.

She turned the knob.

It was time to step into the light.

REENA STEPPED INTO THE EMPTY HALLWAY, LEANING against the wall to catch her breath, her heart pounding crazily in her ears. Finally in the clear, she allowed herself a rare moment of accomplishment.

Not only did she know where Marcus was hiding, but she had rattled Reinhardt and Wells's cage. They would be looking over their shoulders for a long time.

Certainly until Reena could come back and finish the job.

She rubbed the tattoo on her neck, smiling slightly to herself. She might not be able to bring Cruz or her mother back, but she wouldn't let their killers walk away unscathed.

And she wouldn't let Simon rot in jail, either.

Mission accomplished. For now.

She was turning to leave when she heard footsteps gallop toward her down the hall.

INSIDE THE BEDROOM, REINHARDT AND WELLS poured stiff drinks. Walking to the large window overlooking the terraced lawns of the Starling estate, they peered out into the darkness.

"What did she say to you?" Reinhardt asked the senator.

Wells finished his drink in a single gulp. "She said the next time she sees me, she's going to kill me."

———

"AVA! SHAY!" REENA SAID, SURPRISED TO SEE THEM around the corner of the hall. "What are you doing here? Why aren't you waiting in the car?"

"It's Jane," Ava explained. "She knows who she is. We need to find her before she exposes herself to Reinhardt."

Reena shook her head. "I haven't seen her."

"Where the hell is she?" Shay said.

Suddenly, the hallway linen closet burst open. A tall, good-looking guy emerged wearing an expensive suit.

"Jon?" Ava said, mouth open.

He started down the hall, Jane flung over his shoulder. "Jane was just leaving. Let's go."

CHAPTER FIFTY-EIGHT

As the gala shows signs of waning, Jane leaves Shay behind in the car and moves through security, flashing them an irresistible smile. One of the guards, Steve, with a thick neck and thicker mustache, is happy to grant Jane entry. As she goes, he nudges the arm of another man working security next to him.

"That one's easy on the eyes, ain't she? Must be one of Reinhardt's girls."

"Something like that," Jon says, patting Steve on the back.

Jon follows Jane inside, hanging back just enough to not garner her attention. He waits outside her bedroom door, wondering if she's remembering.

And if so, what it's doing to her.

He's patient, in no hurry. This is his mission.

Still, he knows that Ava is in the vicinity and he desperately wants to see her again. To tell her that he's all right. To explain where he's been and why he hasn't contacted her.

But that's not all. He wants to tell her that he's missed her. God, how he's missed her.

The kiss on the porch had been a revelation. It had just taken him some time and distance to figure out what it meant.

But right now his mission is to keep Jane safe.

It's a mission that's compromised when she walks out of her bedroom and heads apprehensively toward Reinhardt's master suite.

She's going to see her father.

But Jon can't let that happen. Not yet. Not tonight.

He removes a small cloth and a tiny vial of chloroform from his jacket, offering Jane a silent apology for what he's about to do.

Then he rushes toward her, grabbing her from behind and covering her mouth with the rag as she moves to open the door to Reinhardt's bedroom.

Moments later, she slumps against him. He flings her over his shoulder in a fireman's carry and steps into the linen closet, closing them off, keeping Jane out of harm's way.

CHAPTER FIFTY-NINE

THE TEAM RACED THROUGH THE VINEYARD TO-
ward Marie's parked car, trying to stay in the shadows just
in case Reinhardt and Wells had a change of heart.

"Where have you been?" Reena asked Jon as they ran
down the grassy hill leading to the road.

It was a question Ava had planned to ask, but now that it
was out, she had another one. "Are you the one who killed
Cain?"

"There'll be time for that later," Shay said as they hit the
road. His knowing glance at Jon wasn't lost on Ava.

"Wait . . . Shay, you knew Jon was alive? You knew where
he was the whole time?"

Shay reached in his pocket for the keys to the car. "I'll explain everything later."

The group piled into the car, Shay driving, Jane in the
passenger seat. Ava slid in the backseat between Reena
and Jon.

As Shay started the car, Ava looked up at Jon.

He held her gaze, his eyes burning into hers through the
darkness. He took her face in his hands and kissed her.

————

THE PLANE WAS ALREADY WAITING WHEN THEY AR-rived at the isolated field sheltered by towering oaks. They weren't done. That would come later, the next time they returned to Napa Valley.

Now it was time to go back to the only place they had left to call home.

Rebun Island.

Ava looked up at Jon. "The kiss was a nice touch, but you still have a lot of explaining to do."

He sighed, giving her a weary smile. "It's a long flight. And we have all the time in the world."

They stood there, looking at each other in the light from the plane, newly hesitant. Despite their moment in the car, the night had done nothing if not prove how dangerous revenge can be. A lot went right, but almost everything that went wrong did so because emotion got in the way.

Still, there would be plenty of time for thinking. Plenty of time for reason.

Now was not that time, Ava decided, putting her arms on Jon's strong shoulders and pulling him in for an embrace. She buried her face in his neck.

"I missed you," she whispered.

He leaned back, looking at her with tenderness as he brushed the hair from her face.

"So come on, let's hear it. Where have you been?" Reena demanded as they marched toward the plane.

Before he could answer, a Lincoln Town Car pulled into the field, screeching to a halt in front of them.

They turned as one, immediately on guard, prepared to fight as a team.

A sharply dressed man emerged from the car, tall and proud. *"Deshis."*

"Takeda?" Reena said.

He walked slowly toward them. "I hear you have had an eventful night," he said. "I hope you have learned that you still have some distance to travel to master the art of revenge."

"Yes, Sensei," Ava said as the others nodded.

"I'm sorry, Sensei," Reena added.

Ava had to a stifle a laugh at Reena's newly submissive tone.

Takeda studied them quietly. "Training commences first thing tomorrow," he said, turning for the plane.

Ava looked from Jon to Takeda and back to Jon again.

"Is that whom you've been with all along?" she asked Jon. "Takeda?"

Jon nodded.

"Seriously, Jon," Reena says as they boarded the plane. "What happened to you?"

Jon looked at them. Then he took a deep breath and started talking.

Jon bursts into the alley behind Tavern Red, surrounded by a Dumpster and cheap fencing. He looks around, the air still and murky, but he doesn't see Cain anywhere.

He does feel something, however: a gun, pressed forcefully against the back of his head.

"Don't shoot," he says. This is not the way he wants to go out.

"It's too late for that," Cain responds, pushing the gun's barrel harder against Jon's head. "You came here looking for this, didn't you? Wanting to die."

"What are you talking about?" Jon asks, trying to formulate a plan for overtaking him.

"That's the only explanation," Cain says. "Because coming here was suicide."

"Actually, that wasn't the idea," Jon says as a few stray cats scatter from under the Dumpster.

"It's okay," Cain says. "I understand more than you think. As long as you kill me it doesn't matter what happens to you, am I right? Because at least then you'll be free from the pain of having put her in harm's way. Must be tough, living with that guilt." Cain cocks the trigger behind him. "At least you won't have to for much longer."

Jon braces himself, prepares to die. Maybe in the next life he'll be able to do things differently.

Maybe.

A moment later, thunder cracks through the air as a bullet is fired. Jon prepares to feel the impact, prepares for darkness. But all he hears is a thump in the ensuing silence.

He opens his eyes in time to see Cain stagger, holding a hand to a gushing wound in his chest. Jon barely has time to register the strange turn of events before Cain topples over, falling onto the concrete with a dull thud.

Jon turns around, expecting to see one of his revenge partners. The person standing there shocks him to the core.

"Takeda?"

Takeda tucks the gun into his dark blue suit jacket and

steps over Cain's body, which is seeping blood like a leaky faucet. Jon can't believe he's actually gone.

And his sensei is actually here.

"I don't understand."

"And you don't have to," Takeda tells him. "All you need to do is trust me. Something you didn't do when deciding to come here. Now come."

"I just wanted to make them pay," Jon explains as Takeda leads him to the black Lincoln.

Takeda stops at the vehicle. "There is a difference between revenge and redemption."

"What's the difference?"

Takeda opens the door for him. "Revenge is an act. Redemption lives solely in the heart. Only when you forgive yourself for what happened will you be able to truly focus."

Jon nods. "What do I do until then?"

"Get in the car and I'll show you," Takeda says.

Jon looks around. The alley is barren and still, but inside the pub, Jon knows a war is raging, the sounds of fighting and breaking glass making their way outside. He imagines Ava, inside and in need of help, and wants to be the one to protect her.

He shakes his head, moving toward the back entrance to Tavern Red. "We have to help them."

Takeda grabs his arm. "Your assistance is not necessary. Another version of you is inside. He will help them." Takeda gets in the car, looking up at Jon. "We have a new mission now."

CHAPTER SIXTY

THE SCORCHED SUN ROSE DUTIFULLY OVER NAPA Valley as the small propeller plane took off, this time in the capable hands of Takeda's personal pilot.

The vast estates and châteaus below became glittery specks as the plane ascended, the green fields and purple vineyards fading into a quiltlike blanket.

Ava watched it all with a mixture of relief and sadness. Napa would always have part of her heart, but this good-bye was different from the last one.

Better.

Maybe Emily Thorne was right. Maybe Ava would sleep more soundly now.

She felt the warm clasp of fingers and looked down to see Jon's hand entwined with hers. They exchanged a smile.

He might help her sleep better, too.

There was still so much about him that she didn't know, but right now, she was just glad he was there.

"So what happened after you left with Takeda?" she asked. "What was the mission?"

"And why are we going back to Japan instead of going to Sacramento to relocate Marcus?" Reena chimed in.

Jon glanced at Takeda, sitting serenely in his seat. Their sensei nodded, giving Jon permission to disclose the truth.

The run-down Thai restaurant sporting the words LU'S PAL-ACE on a faded yellow awning sits on a seedy street near downtown Sacramento. Above the eatery, a beleaguered gentleman who's seen and done too much eats beans from a can as he sits on a springy Murphy bed inside a tight studio apartment.

Looking around, he realizes again that he picked the wrong time to grow a conscience.

He watches wavy television on an old set, waiting for the day to turn to night, the night to turn to day. It's a terrible way to exist, but it's all he can manage while looking over his shoulder every minute of every day, a habit he'd love to break if only he could afford to.

A knock at the door causes him to jump. It's the kind of knock that has intent behind it, something he knows from personal experience.

Except that when he was the one knocking, it meant the person who answered the door wouldn't live to open another.

The man stands, readying himself for what's to come. He could hide, but that would only delay the inevitable. Maybe it's time to let go.

He opens the door, unsurprised to see Jon, one of Cain's hired guns. The man is surprised, however, to see that Jon is accompanied by an older Asian gentleman.

"Darren Marcus?" Jon asks.

The man nods. "I recognize you. Worked for Cain a couple years back, right?"

Jon was too low on the totem pole to remember the man. That's one of the ways Cain kept his hold over you. Kept you awake.

Marcus, feeble and anxious, just needs to know. "Are you here to kill me?"

Jon looks at Takeda, who briefed him on the ride over. "No. We're here to save you."

"So then you already moved Marcus?" Ava shook her head. "That means you knew where he was all along. You didn't need Reena to infiltrate that meeting at all."

Another test. Like the thief on Rebun Island, but on a much grander scale.

"I don't believe it," Ava murmured.

"So Cruz died for a test?" Reena interrupted, cold fury written on her face.

"It wasn't all a test," Shay explained. "We needed to shake Reinhardt and Wells's foundation by ruining Charlie, by severing their relationship. Now it's each man for himself, and that makes them all much more vulnerable."

Takeda moved into the seat next to Reena.

"It is true that I knew of your plans. And true as well that Shay was told you were coming." He paused. "But in revenge, things can be messy. Chaotic. Lethal. You—all of you—must be prepared for that. It is possible to blame me for Cruz's death, if blame is what you seek. But it is also possible that had you finished your training, Cruz would still be alive. As for me, I choose to believe that regret is a waste of energy when one has done one's best. This was the life Cruz chose. And he died the way he wanted to, protecting the woman he loved."

Reena nodded, surprisingly humble. "How long have you known?" she asked. "Did you leave the door to the secret room open to see if we would take our files? Was that part of the test as well?"

Takeda gave her a small smile. "I'll leave that up to you to decide."

The trainees stand in the meditation room, poring over the information on their enemies. The bulky antique mirror hangs on the wall, large enough to see everything yet not imposing enough to be an eyesore.

On the other side of the mirror, Takeda stands, watching his disobedient apprentices intently, none of them the wiser.

Ava approaches her side of the mirror, staring at her reflection. After a moment of soulful silence, she speaks a single word.

No, not a word. A declaration.

"Fukushuu."

Takeda smiles, noting the conviction in her stare, the desire for vengeance etched in her large, angry eyes.

He smiles slightly to himself. She may not be ready yet, but Takeda can see that when she is, nothing—and no one—will be able to get in Ava Winters's way.

CHAPTER SIXTY-ONE

JANE STIRRED AWAKE, GRASPING SHAY'S HAND AS the plane bounced over a pocket of air.

For a moment, she didn't know where she was or what was happening, still swimming up from the oblivion of sleep. But when her gaze came to rest on Shay, she somehow knew she was safe.

"It's okay," he whispered. "We're heading back."

Her eyes traveled to the welt on his head. "Oh God," she says softly. "Does it hurt? I'm sorry, Shay, I just—"

He stopped her. "I get it, Jane. You needed to figure out who you were. Who you are."

She nodded, looking into his eyes. "Did you really hold my hand while I was unconscious last year?"

He looked away, as if the weight of her stare was too much for him to bear. "Every day."

Jane smiled.

He glanced back at her and grinned. "If I'd known you were going to knock me unconscious, I might have reconsidered."

She laughed a little, gently touching the skin around his wound. "I am sorry for this." She blushed. "But I'm also sorry for ruining . . . well, you know."

She had a flash of her hands in his hair, pulling his lips onto hers in the darkened car, an untapped well of emotion and desire rising in the heat of their kiss.

"I thought it was just a distraction," he said.

Jane gave him a knowing smile. "I *had* to go into the estate. But I didn't *want* to."

He held her gaze until she could hardly breathe, the promise of a new beginning in his eyes.

She gestured to the aisle of the plane. "I'm going to . . . ?"

He nodded, standing to let her pass.

She stepped into the aisle and sat next to Takeda. "Sensei," she said, feeling an unexpected rush of affection for the man who had become like a father to her. "I've learned so much. About my identity. My past."

Takeda nodded, looking intently at her.

"It's just . . ." She hesitated. Did she really want the answer to her question? Could she survive it?

"Yes?"

"Was my father involved in my accident?"

Takeda's stare tells her all she needs to know.

She exhales, her heart wrapped in a vise. "So he was in the car that pummeled me. My own father . . ." She turned her eyes on Takeda. "Why would he do that to me?"

"You will learn more in the next phase of your training, Mira."

"No," she protested vehemently. "Mira Reinhardt is dead."

She stood, walking to an empty row of seats to sit by herself. She knew the answer to her question now. She wanted answers. She could survive them.

More than that, she could embrace them. And she would.

Seventeen-year-old Mira Reinhardt lies in a hospital room, unconscious atop the white sheets. Her face and body are covered in massive bruises and layers of bandages. Where her scar will someday reside sits a particularly ghastly and grotesque set of staples, holding her face together while it heals. She's in terrible shape, but the young doctor explains that there is always hope.

He stands next to Takeda, who looks over the young woman struggling to avoid stepping onto the welcome mat of death's door.

"She's certainly a fighter," the doctor says.

"She will be," Takeda says with certainty.

The doctor shakes his head. "Tragic. Especially since they still haven't found out who did it."

"There were no witnesses?" Takeda asks, already knowing the answer.

According to the police reports, the girl was walking home from an art class when the car slammed into her from behind.

Standard, random hit-and-run.

But Takeda knows that when it comes to the people surrounding William Reinhardt, nothing is random.

It's calculated. Coordinated.

The doctor is surprised Takeda is asking these questions. From the way he's dressed, the doctor assumes Takeda is one of the detectives who have been in and out of the room since they brought the girl in.

"I'm a friend," Takeda says, fixated on Mira's still-beating heart, illustrated in green peaks and valleys on the EKG machine by her bed.

"What kind of friend?" the doctor asks.

Takeda reaches into his pocket and withdraws an envelope. He hands it to the doctor.

"What is this?" The doctor bends his head, opening it.

"Does it still matter who I am?" Takeda asks.

The doctor stares at the money inside the envelope before stuffing it into his pocket.

"What do you want?" he asks Takeda.

"Tell the girl's father that she's dead," Takeda instructs. "That she never woke up."

The doctor is clearly perplexed. "Why would you want me to do that?"

"Because in doing so, you'll be saving her life," Takeda says, knowing that Reinhardt won't stop until his daughter is dead.

And Takeda won't let that happen.

The girl still has so much to live for. And so much to avenge.

CHAPTER SIXTY-TWO

"How did it feel to finally face the one who wronged you?" Takeda asked Ava.

They were halfway home, halfway to Rebun Island. Ava was tired but grateful for the long flight. It was a comforting kind of limbo between Napa and Japan. Between what had happened and what was to come. Who they were and who they would be.

"It felt right," Ava said after thinking about it. "Like I was restoring balance."

Takeda nodded. "Exactly as it should."

Ava sat back in her seat. "I just can't believe that Reinhardt arranged to have my grandmother killed," she said. "That someone close to me and to my grandmother herself, was behind it." She looked to Takeda for answers. "Why would Marie want to hurt my grandmother? To steal Starling from me?"

Takeda shook his head. "Even I am surprised by this revelation," he said. "Are you certain Charlie wasn't lying? Attempting to alleviate his own guilt by blaming another?"

"I don't think so. It makes a strange kind of sense. How else would someone know exactly how to play me? Exactly

246

what it would take to steal the vineyard? I just don't understand why Marie would betray my grandmother. Why would
she go to such lengths to ruin my family?"

Takeda considered. "In my experience, a lack of logic often points to something more . . . personal."

Ava nodded. "You're right. It does feel personal."

"What will you do?" Takeda asked.

Ava looked into his eyes. "Find out why she did it. And
then make her pay."

She turned her head to the window. Charlie was just the
beginning. Her revenge path was far from over.

CHAPTER SIXTY-THREE

A WINGED WARRIOR GLIDED GRACEFULLY THROUGH the sky as Ava stood on the edge of the cliff. She watched the bird soar.

A starling, perhaps?

She'd like to think so. It would be fitting.

Opening her hand, she looked at the cork souvenir in her palm. It was one of the few items she had brought with her, one of the mementos in the satchel hidden in the wall. Looking back, it was easy to see why she had chosen it for her journey. It had been the perfect reminder of the person she'd been, the past that had once grounded her like an anchor in a strong wind.

But like the piece of Acala's flame, she didn't need it anymore.

She knew who she was now. Knew where she was headed. Most of all she knew she was strong enough for whatever lay ahead. That she would adapt.

And prevail.

A cool breeze blew in off the channel, like a silent sign that it was time.

Time to let go. Time to move on.

She didn't hesitate. She just lifted her arm and threw the souvenir out over the cliff. It spun end over end, glinting in the sunlight as it sailed toward the deep blue sea.

She felt lighter already.

Another bird flew overhead, then another. Soon a whole flock of them soared past. Like they were welcoming her home.

The sound of rocks crunching underfoot pulled her attention from the birds. She turned to find Jane approaching from the tera. She stood next to Ava and looked out over the water. When she finally spoke her voice was soft but sure.

"When I was training with Takeda, right after I came out of my coma, they flew by me, too. Now I wonder if they were starlings."

Ava smiled at her. "I don't know. They're too far away to be sure, but I like to think they are."

"Ava . . . ," Jane began, "I'm so sorry. For what my father did to you, for not knowing that everything I had came at your expense." She shook her head. "I was so stupid."

Ava squeezed her arm. "He was your father. And love is blind. I know that better than most people."

"Still," Jane said, shaking her head, "I can't believe that all that time, I was in your house, your room . . ."

"I'd planned to raise my daughter in that room one day." Ava turned to her. "Who knows, maybe she would have carved her initials next to mine."

Jane could only stare.

A few minutes passed before Ava spoke again. "You'll figure it all out. I promise."

"How do you know?"

Ava looks at her resolutely. "Because I'll help you."

They looked back out at the sea, shielding their eyes against the sun. A few dark sleeper fish rose above the waters before falling back into the abyss.

A few minutes later, Jon ambled up behind them.

"Hey," he said.

But his tone was too casual. Ava was starting to know him. She could tell he had something on his mind.

Jane seemed to hear it, too.

"Well, I'll see you guys at training." She jogged off, leaving them alone.

It was strange to be back on the cliff with Jon. They had met here so many times before, but this time, it felt different. They had both changed. Both adapted. Both evolved.

A long silence settled between them. Ava began to wonder if she was wrong. Maybe Jon had just come to look at the sea.

"Come on," she said, turning to leave. "We should go, too."

Jon stepped in front of her, their bodies close. "I owe you an explanation, Ava. About my time working for Cain."

She shook her head. "You don't owe me anything."

"It's just . . ." He paused with a sigh. "I'm no saint."

"I never asked you to be," she said. "I just asked you to be honest."

Jon took a deep breath. "I know. And I want to do that now. It's long overdue."

Jon sits in his Pontiac Firebird in a charmingly idyllic suburb of Napa Valley, where even the least decadent of homes dwarfs most real estate in the country. Towering houses define the block; luscious lemon trees line the sidewalks. The streetlamps are somewhat antiquated, providing subtle ambience. It's beautiful and quaint.

But Jon's not here by choice.

He's been camped out for hours, the gun Cain had given him sitting on his lap. It weighs only a few pounds, but somehow it manages to crush every fiber of his being. He looks out the window, spotting a candy-apple-red Mustang, just as Cain described, pulling up in front of a large German Colonial across the street.

Jon's palms are so sweaty he can barely wrap his hands around the trigger as he lifts the gun.

This is it. Cain needs him to send a message to the girl in the car by putting a bullet in her boyfriend's back. Jon doesn't know their names. Didn't ask. It's going to be hard enough to do this as it is.

He hears the young couple's laughter from across the street, although he can't hear what they're saying. Jon looks at the gun as it shimmers in the darkness. He's never shot anyone, doesn't even like to put mousetraps out in his and Courtney's apartment.

He looks back at the young couple silhouetted in the car. He can't do it. The money isn't worth it, even if it is a cool ten grand.

He'll give it back. He doesn't want it.

Jon takes out the disposable he carries for emergencies and complications, both of which Cain doesn't care for. His hands tremble as he dials Cain's direct line.

After a few rings, Cain finally answers. "I take it you're not calling with good news."

"How do you know that?"

"I've been doing this a long time, kid."

Jon hesitates, looks at the young lovers, embracing against the side of the car. They kiss sweetly before heading inside. It seals the deal for Jon.

"I'm sorry," he says to Cain. "I can't do it. I'm sorry I wasted your time."

Cain is unfazed. "I'm not the one you need to apologize to. It's your fiancée, Courtney,"

Jon grows dim, uneasy. Hearing Cain utter Courtney's name is the last thing Jon expects.

Or wants.

"How do you know about Courtney?"

"I make it my business to know everything about the people who work for me. For unfortunate times just like these." He pauses. "It's Tuesday, right? Courtney stays late at work on Tuesdays. Someone should tell her that shortcut she takes home isn't very safe. Especially tonight."

"What are you going to do?" Jon asks, dread flooding his body.

"If you do the job you were hired to do, nothing," Cain says. "But if you don't fire that gun within the next twenty minutes, another one will be going off. And it will be aimed at your fiancée. Your choice."

"I thought I could get to her before they did," he explained, staring out over the channel. "Turns out, I was wrong."

Ava didn't know what to say.

"I know now that I can't hold on to it—to her—forever. I'm not the one who killed Courtney. They are. I think I'm finally coming to terms with that. It's time to move on."

"I'm glad that Cain's death helped you realize that," Ava said softly.

"Cain's death had nothing to do with it," he said, looking at her.

"Then what?"

"It was you." He pulled her into his arms. "That kiss on the porch in Napa. The way I couldn't forget about you even when we were apart. It made me realize that there's more to life than guilt and anger. Even for someone like me."

He lowered his face to hers, their lips almost meeting. But now wasn't the time. The sun was rising.

And they had work to do.

"You ready?" he asked her, the question lingering in the air.

Flashing him a smile, Ava turned, running toward the training grounds. She looked back at him.

"Well? What are you waiting for?"

They fell into line with Reena and Jane. Shay stood in front with Takeda, both men surveying the slightly smaller group, their numbers diminished by one. Ava glanced at Reena, knowing how hard it must be for her friend to be here without Cruz.

Reena met her eyes, understanding moving between them. They were sisters now.

Sisters in revenge.

They might not always see eye to eye, but they would have each other's backs until the end.

She took Reena's hand as Jane grabbed hers.

Shay cleared his throat, paving the way for Takeda to speak.

"It is time to continue where we left off. Time to resume your training. Time to take back your lives."

"And something tells me I think you'll all be ready this time," Shay said, his nonchalance undercutting Takeda's seriousness.

"We are ready, Sensei," the group said in unison.

"Then the next time you return to the States, you will have greater skill. You will be more capable. You will be fully prepared for revenge."

His gaze settled on Ava. She was ready. To learn. To prepare. Like Acala, she had burned off her weaknesses. Because when you've lost everything, sometimes there is nothing left but revenge.

And the next time Ava Winters returns to Napa Valley, it will be to reclaim her empire.

EPILOGUE

In room 402 of the ICU at St. Luke's Hospital, Courtney lies still in her bed, the flowers on the bedside table wilting. The EKG emits a constant string of steady beeps that offer little more than hope.

Then, abruptly, the beeping grows louder, and Courtney's eyes open to the dimly lit room. She stares at the ceiling, a look of disbelief on her once-frozen face.

She's awake. Alive.

Daniella watches from the shadows of the room as Courtney wakes from her extended slumber. Marie's daughter can't help but smile. Courtney's recovery represents yet another way to wreak havoc on the life of the girl who always had everything while Daniella and her mother scraped by, living off Ava's hand-me-downs and Sylvie's charity.

Daniella had Ava Winters dethroned once.

And she'll do anything to keep her from reclaiming the keys to her kingdom.

ACKNOWLEDGMENTS

First and foremost I want to thank Mike Kelley and Melissa Loy for your unwavering support, and for creating a world you so generously allowed me to play in and expand upon. Sunil Nayar and the entire *Revenge* writing staff for your constant encouragement. Andrew Bick for your photography skills. Sonja Wright, thank you for all your help. Everyone at ABC, you have all been beyond gracious and obliging. Laura B. Hopper, thank you for your invaluable guidance. My management team—Zadoc Angell, Matt Horwitz, Dave Brown—along with Lev Ginsberg, for always being in my corner. Thank you to my incredibly loving parents and sister who forever believe in me. Finally, Danielle, my love, your endless strength and support go beyond words.

ABOUT THE AUTHOR

Jesse Lasky grew up on Long Island, before going to college in upstate New York. After graduation he moved to Manhattan to work on various television and film projects. He currently lives in Los Angeles and works on the writing staff of ABC's *Revenge*.